A NURSE
FOR THE
WOLFMAN

EVE LANGLAIS

Chimera Secrets 1 - Romantic Horror

PROLOGUE

THE AMBUSH CAME OUT OF NOWHERE. ENEMY soldiers rose from hidden trenches, their guns rapidly firing at the convoy on a mission to deliver goods—clothing and medical equipment to a refugee camp.

Luke's training took over. He immediately jumped out of the back of the truck and rolled under it for cover. He poked the muzzle of his gun out and began shooting in the general direction of the attackers.

For a while the rapid staccato of gunfire filled the air, along with the sharp yells, screams, and sobs of those injured. He couldn't tell if they were winning or about to be overrun. In that moment, only survival counted. And Luke was good at surviving against the odds.

A kid bounced around in the foster system because of druggie parents quickly learned how to evade danger. He might not have gotten good grades in school, but he graduated with life skills. With graduation came his ticket out of foster care, but unlike many, he didn't end up on the streets, turning tricks or doing petty crimes to survive. He joined the army. A steady paycheck, medical benefits, and a chance to serve his country. Smartest thing he ever did.

Problem was all those fancy recruitment posters didn't mention the part he'd be serving it on foreign soil fighting the very people they'd been tasked with saving.

But it wasn't up to him to figure out the politics, or even if he fought on the right side. Luke went where he was told. Served like a good soldier. Learned to kill, too, which proved easier than expected.

As the gunfire died, he rolled in the dust and dirt and popped to his feet. Rifle aimed, looking for movement. The air held a haze that stung the eyes and tickled the lungs.

He ignored the moans of his injured comrades as he took slow and measured steps toward the hump of rock and packed dirt that hid one of the shooters. He learned early on to never assume the enemy was dead and done.

As Luke approached, he kept his gaze focused, his gun held upright, finger on the trigger. He prepared to fire as he neared the outcropping, only to ease out a breath when he saw the body on the other side. The third eye rimmed in red meant the man wouldn't rise again.

Turning, he saw his buddy, Jorge, nudging another corpse—a rather corpulent one—with the toe of his boot. "This one doesn't have a gun."

"Maybe he was throwing rocks," joked Luke. It did seem odd, which should have been the first clue. "How—"

He never did finish his sentence. The voluminous robes suddenly birthed a smaller figure, just a boy. Which meant they both hesitated.

They knew better.

The missing gun was in the child's hand. Before Jorge or Luke could react, the child was screaming and firing, spraying bullets wildly.

Luke knew he was fucked the moment the bullet shattered his hip. A soldier who couldn't run wasn't much good on the battlefield. He almost welcomed the second and third bullets. They took him from searing into darkness, a darkness that spat him back out into painful reality.

He regained consciousness as medics swarmed the area, quickly rolling him onto a stretcher, carrying him to safety.

How am I not dead? A miracle surely. Despite his lower body not responding at all, except to hurt, he held on to a shred of hope. The doctor dashed it with one look.

"His entire pelvis is fucked. His arm is hanging by a tendril of muscle. We can't fix him. Clean and wrap his wounds then get him prepped for shipment back to the States." The fate of those no longer suitable for fighting.

Still, they'd made great strides in medicine.

The doctors back home did their best. Stitched his

arm back together and kept him from losing it. His thumb and one finger still worked. Swapped out his broken pelvis for an artificial one. But they couldn't repair the nerve damage. All the rehab in the world didn't get rid of his pronounced limp, his crippled fingers, the pain.

He began to pop pills. What else did he have to do all day? The military gave him an honorable discharge and not much else.

Fuck you very much.

He wished he'd died in the fight like Jorge had. His friend never made it out of the hospital, and there were days Luke thought him the lucky one. What did he have to live for? The nightmares of that day played over and over again. The faces of those he'd killed haunting him, fingers pointing, saying, "You deserve this."

Maybe he did. Maybe living was his punishment.

About a year after his return, the knock on his shitty apartment door barely roused him from his drunken stupor.

When the pounding continued, he managed a slurred, "Fuck off and go away."

Instead, the door was kicked open and a beast of a guy in a suit two sizes too small, wearing shades and a scowl, entered.

"What the fuck?" Luke exclaimed.

"Are you Luke Harris?"

"So what if I am? You ain't got the right to come

busting in here." Especially since the guy didn't have a badge.

The fellow stepped aside so that another man in a suit could enter.

Luke immediately disliked him, with his perfectly cut hair and smooth-shaven jaw. "Hello, Private Harris."

"Don't 'hello' me. What the hell you thinking, busting into my place?" he snarled.

"Excuse my employee's enthusiasm. Bruno can be a little impatient."

"I don't give a rat's ass what Bruno is. You can both get the fuck out."

"Don't be too hasty, Private Harris."

"How do you know my name? You work for the government? Come to evaluate me and see how much more of my disability you can cut?"

"I'm not a state or federal employee. My name is Doctor Chimera."

A doctor? Here? Why? Luke's gaze narrowed. "You going to fake a report saying I'm not crippled so the military cuts me off?" It wouldn't surprise him. He had a hard enough time getting the benefits he was entitled to. Agencies kept trying to claw them back.

"Again, I don't work for the government, or the military. I am here because I read your file. I think we can help each other."

Luke snorted. "Now I know you're full of shit. What do you want?"

"To offer you a second chance."

"Chance for what? If you read my file, then you know I'm a cripple." He slapped his thigh and barely felt it. Some days, he could barely drag himself across his apartment to grab another beer.

"What if I said we could fix your injuries? Make you better than before."

"I'd say you're full of shit."

The man in the suit smiled. "Five years ago, I was in a wheelchair with even less mobility than you." He turned and did a two-step. "That changed after my treatment."

"You got robot legs under there?" Luke asked, his interest piqued. A cyborg body wasn't his first choice, but he wouldn't say no either.

"Flesh and blood," the doctor assured. "We don't replace the damage; we actually fix it. And our treatment can fix you, too."

Suspicion was part of his nature, hence why Luke frowned and said, "What's the catch?"

"No catch and no cost to you. We require suitable subjects who wouldn't mind experimental treatment."

"Not FDA approved, eh?" He snorted. "Neither is half the shit I snort. So what do you need from me?"

"Permission. Sign these forms authorizing us to handle your medical care."

Luke eyed the several-page document Bruno handed him. "For how long?"

"As long as it takes to make you whole again."

"Does it hurt?"

The doctor shrugged. "Yes. But no worse than

you've suffered. And really, with these kinds of result..." The guy glanced down at his legs.

To be able to walk again and not drag. To taste freedom rather than the cloying closeness of these four walls.

"Can I have time to think about it and look this over?" He waved the thick sheaf of paper.

"No. This is a one-time offer, my friend. If you don't want it, then there are plenty of others who will."

"Why me?" Luke wasn't a person whom luck shone upon. In his experience, things usually went from bad to worse.

"You are a healthy male of prime age."

"I'll grant you the age part, but I don't know about healthy." No point in lying about his vices. It would suck to say yes and then get kicked out of the program for the drugs in his blood.

"The narcotics and alcohol in your system can be flushed. You haven't been doing them long enough to do serious damage to your organs."

"Do I have to stay in a hospital?"

"A clinic, yes. In the mountains. You'll have your own room. Three meals a day plus snacks."

"Hot nurses?"

Dr. Chimera's lips quirked. "Some are attractive, yes."

"I don't know." It sounded all too good to be true. "If I go, what about my apartment, my stuff?"

"Your things can be put in storage. And you're making excuses. Do you want to walk again?"

"Yes." With every fiber of his being.

"Then accept my offer now or stay here." The curled lip as the man looked around filled Luke with anger—and shame. He knew what Chimera saw. Filth. Squalor. The apartment of a guy who'd given up.

"What if it doesn't work?"

Again, the small tight smile. "It will work. Do we have a deal, Private Harris?"

Given the choice, a chance to return to the man he was or drink himself to death, he chose hope.

Luke held out his hand. "Let's do this."

It was the worst decision he ever made.

CHAPTER ONE

I HOPE I MADE THE RIGHT DECISION. TODAY Margaret started a new job, one that would take her away from the city she knew. Away from everything, including civilization.

A helicopter was required to reach the remote clinic she'd been hired to work for. How situating an establishment out of reach by normal means made sense, she couldn't have said. Usually clinics were places of healing, accessible to all who might need them.

Then again, this was a special place. A place that required her signature on page after page of contracts and legal jargon about non-disclosures, enough writing her hand cramped. The smudge of ink as Chimaeram Clinic's human resources fingerprinted her and ran a background check told of the seriousness of the job. But all the inconveniences in the world didn't matter, not when she saw what they offered.

Six figures for six months work, with the possibility of extending the contract if things worked out.

Only an idiot would say no. Nurses didn't make big bucks in publicly funded hospitals. Not in Canada at least. Depending on the promises the government in power made, nursing hours could be cut. She might find herself scrambling to make ends meet with no notice.

Margaret jumped at the chance of real money, and to embark on a new start. Having recently come out of a nasty relationship where her ex-boyfriend had the nerve to accuse her—rather than the fact he slept with his coworker—of being the problem, Margaret found herself wanting some peace and quiet. Especially since Jeremy wouldn't leave her alone. Apparently, she wasn't supposed to dump him. She was being unreasonable. A bitch.

She couldn't disagree with the latter. She had no time or use for cheaters. But the asshole just wouldn't go away. So she would.

Given the length of time she'd be gone, Margaret packed up the things she wanted to keep and put them in storage. She sold and gave away the accumulated crap she didn't care about. The only things she brought with her to the clinic were two large suitcases and a purse. Not a ton of clothes, given she'd packed a warm winter jacket, which took up a lot of space; however, she wouldn't have to worry about work apparel. Apparently, the clinic provided a uniform—and laundry services. Another perk.

With her on this voyage to the unknown was another woman, Becky—also a nurse—with a much more loquacious personality and the type of bubbly chatter that made Margaret wish for duct tape. A good thing the headsets provided allowed her some relief from the talking.

As the helicopter slipped between two mountain peaks, she was struck anew at the stark beauty of the location. The Rockies were a wild and untamed place for the most part. Sure, there were a few scattered towns, small settlements with limited populations. But they at least had roads and stores to reach them.

The clinic didn't.

It worried her a little that she wouldn't be able to leave. There was no calling a cab if things sucked. No ordering in pizza or hitting a movie or even a bar for alcoholic relaxation. The clinic would be her everything for the next little while. It seemed crazy when she thought too long about it. She kept reminding herself it was only for six months.

Despite all the paperwork and questions she'd answered, Margaret still had no idea what to expect. Just an assurance that all her needs would be met. Given the lack of information on the internet about the Chimaeram Clinic, and given the security around it, she assumed it was some kind of government-run, top-secret facility. Which made it rather exciting. Perhaps she'd be witness to a great stride in medical science. Or perhaps it was some kind of rehab center for the rich. She might meet a movie star!

The helicopter swooped into a valley formed by towering peaks, the tops of them white with snow, and yet as they dipped, the frigid temperatures and barren rock changed to lush green with flourishing trees, their tops tall and bushy, with occasional open patches filled with bushes and long grass.

The helicopter swept past the woods into a massive clearing, obviously regularly mown given the scrub on the ground remained low and there wasn't a single sapling to be seen.

The uneven terrain turned into a field of green that appeared to be grass with a dirt track ringing it. Man-made for sure.

A poke in her arm had her turning to see her companion gesturing, her lips moving.

Margaret frowned. Becky grinned and tapped her window.

Craning to peek via the window opposite her, Margaret noticed the crystal-clear waters of a lake and, within in it, moving shapes. Fish that darted erratically as the shadow of the helicopter darkened their habitat and stirred up waves. On the other side of the lake, a concrete pad with a giant X for landing awaited. Farther beyond, a squat building of only two stories ringed by concrete, a few all-terrain vehicles parked next to it.

The chopper alighted with only a slight jolt, and while her companion immediately unbuckled, Margaret waited for the pilot to speak through their headset. "You may disembark."

Only then did she remove the earpieces that protected her from the sound of the blades and unclip her harness. The door popped open, and Becky hopped out with no fear or regard for the still spinning blades. The fact they were well overhead didn't reassure. Margaret kept a wary eye on the moving metal as she emerged more slowly, the tube rails providing steps down to the ground.

Now what? As Margaret stood there, hugging herself, noticing the chilly bite of wind, she felt some trepidation. This place was literally in the middle of nowhere. No roads. No power lines. A single building, surely not large enough to do everything it promised.

What had she gotten herself into?

The pilot emerged on the opposite side of the chopper, and she heard thumping as he removed their baggage. She clutched her purse tight, only partially comforted by the cell phone inside. It wouldn't have any signal, and yet she couldn't leave it behind.

A vehicle zipped toward them, similar to a golf cart but with a more rugged appearance and painted black.

The driver appeared very soldier-like with his dark uniform, shaded sunglasses, and granite countenance. When he exited the vehicle, she noted the gun holstered by his side.

It didn't help her anxiety. Why did he need a gun?

What did ease her somewhat was the man in the suit accompanying the guard. The same man who'd interviewed her a few weeks ago. Mr. Lowry, company lawyer and the one lugging around several inches of paperwork for hiring new staff.

"Miss Henley and Miss Frederickson. Delighted to see you again and so glad you chose to join our establishment.

"As if I'd say no," Becky gushed with enthusiasm. "This place is just gorgeous.

Margaret remained more reserved. A woman in her thirties shouldn't be bouncing around like a sugar-intoxicated child. "It's nice to see you again, Mr. Lowry." In his late forties, possibly even his fifties, Lowry was tall, trim, and wore his white hair in a short cut that gave him a scholarly appearance when matched with his small round glasses.

"I trust the trip in was uneventful."

"Epic ride," Becky enthused, her red hair bouncing in time to the syllables. "The air up here is so crisp and fresh."

"Brisk too," he advised. "I do hope you both brought sweaters."

Along with a warm winter coat, boots, gloves, hat, and even a scarf. Margaret's tenure here would end mid-February, so she came prepared.

"I'm sure I'll find a way to keep warm." Becky giggled.

It took effort not to roll her eyes. Margaret had had heard enough chatter before boarding the helicopter to realize Becky was the type who thrived on fraternization.

"If you ladies will accompany me, I'll show you the facility and your quarters."

They climbed into the utility vehicle and sped off toward the only building in sight. A building that better have magical properties when it came to parsing out space given what it supposedly held. Cafeteria, lounge with pool table and televisions for viewing and others for gaming. Suites with private bathrooms. That was just for the staff. Then there were the actual patients themselves.

As if sensing her question, Lowry pointed. "Don't let this building fool you. Most of our facility is underground in order to preserve the natural beauty of this place. We were fortunate that we found a series of interlinked caverns that provided a controlled temperature environment."

"We'll be living in caves?" Margaret's nose wrinkled. She was a person who thrived on daylight.

"Caves only in the basest of terms. I assure you the accommodations are spacious and well appointed."

"With no windows?" Or escape. What if there was a fire?

"Unfortunately, no, however on your off time you are more than welcome to roam the grounds. While we don't recommend swimming in the lake, given the frigid temperature caused by the ice melt, there is an outdoor track if you like to run and an area set up with picnic tables if you wish to take some meals outside."

"What about the woods? Any trails? I am a huge bird watcher," Becky remarked. "I brought my camera to see if I could add to my montage." A surprising hobby given what Margaret knew of her thus far.

"We don't recommend entering them given the ease with which you can get lost. You might also want to restrict your outdoor time to daylight hours."

"Why can't we pop out at night?" Margaret asked.

"What she said," Becky added. "I totally want to check the stars. Can we see the Northern Lights from here?"

"Again, it's not recommended, as it is more difficult to protect you at night."

"Protect us from what?" asked Margaret.

"Wild animals, of course." Lowry partially turned to reply over his shoulder. "Given this location is too remote for most hunters, the natural predators are plentiful. Wolves. Bears. Mountain cats can be dangerous as well." Lowry gestured in the distance.

"They attack people?" It surprised her. Then again, as a city girl, she'd not ever done much with nature.

"This valley is a bit of locked-in ecosystem, so their menu choices are limited. We keep a lookout posted to watch for any that might stray close to the clinic." Lowry pointed to a man on the rooftop of the building.

"Why not cull them if they're dangerous?" Becky asked with blithe ignorance.

Lowry shot her a sharp look. "We don't kill things around here unless there is no other choice."

"Yet your driver is armed with a gun."

"Which is loaded with tranquilizers. Not bullets. Man or beast, our clinic is a place for healing."

Now that they were actually here, Margaret felt comfortable asking, "Healing what and who?"

"You'll soon see," was the cryptic reply as they reached the metal door into the building. Mr. Lowry held up a black card with a golden lion on it. "You'll each receive one of these programmed to access your specific quarters, the common areas, and whatever section you're assigned to work."

"You keep everything locked?" Margaret asked.

"Given industrial espionage is a concern, and the value of the equipment, we feel it is best if we remove temptation."

Margaret didn't point out the fact there was no way to sell information or equipment. Not to mention, she had no interest in snooping. She was here to work and earn a living the honest way.

Lowry ran his access card over a plain black panel. There was a click, and he opened the door. "Ladies." He gestured for them to precede him.

Becky went first with Margaret following, frowning as she noted the square antechamber with its plain gray walls and another door ahead of them. There were ventilation grills in the ceiling and on the walls close to the floor. She also spotted the iris of a camera watching.

But no security guard to sign them in, which surprised her. Then again, who would come here and walk in unannounced?

It took the keycard to get past the next door, and then they were in a hallway with an elevator in front of them and nothing else. Not even doors. Why have a hall? Perhaps to allow the windows at either end to spill in natural daylight?

The elevator proved a decent size, allowing her to move to the back while Becky yapped at Lowry. "How many levels is this place?" Because there were no buttons inside. Just the use of the keycard and Lowry saying, "Habitat level."

"There are two floors above ground and six below," he replied.

"Six?" Margaret queried. "How deep are those caverns?"

"Pretty deep," Lowry admitted as the cabin slowed and the doors slid open. "Welcome to the first level. This is where you'll be housed during your stay."

Exiting, they found themselves in a vast space. To the left, a bunch of trestle tables with benches. Empty for the moment, but the stainless-steel counters beyond them with plastic hoods showed where the buffet started. To the right, scattered couches around a massive television currently playing the latest Marvel superhero movie—still in theatres she should add, yet they were screening it in this remote place. A few people lounged watching it, the silence kind of uncanny given they all wore headsets. Only the occasional chuckle emerged as someone laughed at the antics on screen.

Lowry noted her gaze. "Rather than create a series

of closed-in spaces, we felt it easier to provide headsets to control some of the noise." He waved to a farther screen with La-Z-Boy-type seats and more people concentrating on screens, remotes in hand. "We do our best to provide entertainment. Food as well. You'll find our selection to be varied and excellent. Breakfast is from six a.m. until nine, lunch from eleven until two. And dinner is five to eight."

"What if you need a midnight snack?" Becky added. "I'm a chip-aholic myself."

"There are dispensing machines with snacks and beverages in the corridors where your rooms are situated. They don't actually require any money to use, just make a selection."

"You seem to have thought of everything," Margaret remarked.

"We had to," Lowry confided, giving them a smile. "When confining a large number of people to an area, keeping them content is paramount. It leads to less conflict. Which reminds me, while we don't condone fraternization, we also don't prohibit it. We are conscious that sexual needs require an outlet. But that doesn't mean you have to say yes to anyone who asks. If someone makes unwanted advances and persists after being asked to cease, then please notify me or Mr. Dillinger, who is the human resources manager in charge of dealing with situations."

"How is it dealt with?" Margaret asked.

"A first offense will receive a strongly worded

warning. A second will see the offender fired and removed from the establishment."

Good to know they didn't screw around and reassuring since Margaret had no intention of getting involved with anyone.

As they strode through the room, a few sets of eyes glanced their way. Hands raised in a welcoming salute.

Becky waved enthusiastically back. "You have a lot of hot-looking guys," she noted with absolutely no shame.

"Coincidence, I'm sure," Lowry stated with a smile. "Could also be the fresh air and regular exercise we encourage from all our staff. Healthy minds start with healthy bodies."

Given Margaret was a jogger, she totally agreed. Nothing better than a morning run with crisp morning air filling the lungs.

Exiting the common area, they found themselves at a literal crossroad. Lowry paused and pointed. "To the left are the male quarters. And to our right, female. It should be noted that for the comfort of others, you are restricted to your wing and cannot have guests from the other sections."

"What about the hanky-panky you said we could have?" Becky asked.

A groan remained caught behind the tongue Margaret bit. Did the girl have no shame?

Lowry didn't seem to mind. "We have rooms set aside off the main chamber that can be used."

Sex rooms? Margaret couldn't help a wrinkle of her

nose. Kind of gross, however Becky beamed and clapped her hands. "Epic."

Figured.

"What's straight ahead?" Margaret asked, noticing the third hallway.

"Nothing. The area is undeveloped."

A man with auburn hair and freckles against a tan —that belied the common rule of thumb regarding redheads and sun—approached in track pants and a form-fitting shirt. He gave them a nod of acknowledgement as he moved to head around them, only to halt as Lowry said, "Beckett, do you have a moment?"

"Sure thing, boss." The guy paused by them.

"Do you mind showing what happens when unauthorized personnel attempt to enter the wrong wing?"

"So long as it doesn't get put on my record."

"I'll make sure it doesn't," Lowry promised.

The handsome fellow stepped into the woman's corridor, and the light overhead turned red. A female voice emerged from a speaker the ceiling saying, "Warning. Warning. You are entering a restricted area. Please exit the area immediately."

"They get a warning?" Margaret's voice might have held a hint of mockery.

"The first time. Beckett?" Lowry inclined his head, and the guy sighed.

"Ah, boss, seriously? You know that shit sucks, right?"

"I know, but I want to reassure these ladies that

21

their virtue is safe while they work here. I'll arrange for a bonus on your next check."

"It better be a good one," Beckett grumbled as he stepped back into the corridor. This time while the light flashed red, there was no verbal warning. Just a buzzing sound and then the big man hit the floor.

It took Margaret a long stare before she blinked and said to Lowry, "What just happened?"

Becky understood. "He was zapped." She made a buzzing sound.

"Indeed, he was. Given we take the safety of our staff—especially the sometimes more vulnerable female members—seriously, we have measures in place to ensure the rules are followed. As you noted, a warning is only good if obeyed. We wanted something for the more stubborn rule breakers."

"Seems kind of drastic," Margaret remarked. "How often do you zap your employees?"

A faint smile curved Lowry's lips. "Not often. Usually the infractions we see are more a result of a few too many alcoholic beverages leading people in the wrong direction than actual intent."

"You serve booze?" Becky exclaimed. "Sweet."

"Surprising, I would have said," Margaret added. "Isn't it usually protocol in confined populations to limit or outright prohibit alcohol?"

"Again, this is not a prison. We want our staff to be happy and feel at home. Nothing wrong with a few beers or a glass of wine after a day's work." Lowry had a smooth answer for everything.

This place sounded a little too good to be true. "Do those rules also apply to drugs?"

"Given Canada's stance on marijuana, we do allow its use when off duty but nothing else, as we don't want people to be experiencing psychedelic episodes or dealing with truly addictive substances."

"Is there a manual we can read with all the do's and don'ts?" Margaret planned to read up on the place.

Whereas Becky scoffed. "I just follow one general rule. Don't be a dick."

"Um..." Was there really a reply to that?

Becky laughed. "Oh, your face, girl. It is priceless." She snickered. "My aunt used to say it all the time."

"And it's probably the most encompassing way of saying it. Don't be a dick and you'll be fine. " Lowry chuckled. "Shall we continue? While we don't have a manual per se, we do have a forum you can access that will help you find your way around. The console to access it is in your room which is next on the tour." He waved them ahead once more.

Margaret let Becky skip ahead first, and when she didn't hit the floor beside the still passed out Beckett, she followed, eyeing him as she passed.

"Will he be okay?"

"He'll be fine. Someone will be along shortly to put him to bed. He'll wake in a few hours with no ill effects."

A peek behind showed Lowry following them without setting off the alarm. The rule restricting entry didn't apply to him it seemed. Who else had special dispensation?

The hallway went for quite a distance and branched off a few times. The place was massive. It made her wonder how it got built. Did they fly in all the supplies and equipment? It must have taken years. How did no one notice? Or maybe they did but didn't care.

Lowry stopped in front of a white door marked W21. "This is Miss Frederickson's room." He handed Becky a card. "Your key."

"Sweet." She slapped it on the console and popped in once the door opened. "This is huge," she exclaimed. "And a bed big enough for two."

For a moment, Margaret feared they'd be room-mates, but Lowry pressed a card into her hand. "You are in the next room. Take a moment to look inside."

The door opened onto a bigger space than expected. Large enough to handle a full-sized bed with a nightstand on one side. An oversized plush chair. Even a desk with a stool equipped with a monitor and keyboard.

Lowry pointed. "Your connection to the outside world. We have internet access, so you can check and reply to email. There is also a hookup to the Chimaeram Clinic forum. Ask questions, make friends. Read the rules." Said with a teasing smile.

The fact she could use the internet surprised her. Especially given the security. "Is our usage monitored?"

"Everything on company property is monitored; however, that is only to ensure no one is stealing secrets."

"So don't expect privacy," she murmured, yet couldn't complain. The contract did warn they'd be supervised closely.

"There are no cameras inside the bedrooms or bathrooms. The only things we access when employees are in the privacy of their quarters are messages sent and received."

Seemed fair enough. She wandered deeper into the room and felt a slight huffing breeze. She noted the grill in the ceiling and another by the bottom of the floor. So long as there was power, she wouldn't asphyxiate. Not a good thought to have underground.

Margaret pointed to the bed. "Fresh bedding is..."

"Taken care for you once a week. More often if you request it. We also provide laundry services." Lowry pointed to his left. "That is your bathroom. You'll find basic toiletries in the cabinet under the sink. More are available via the dispensers we passed in the hall." Which were inset into the walls and comprised of a window showing their wares and a dispensing slot at the bottom. "You can also place an order with Marsha, who is in charge of supply management. She is the first door when you enter the women's wing. But it's probably easier to send her a message via the terminal." He waved to the screen.

"What happens if there's an emergency? A fire or

something else?" Margaret did her best to not think about the fact there was no window. No easy escape.

"The whole place is equipped with fire extinguishers." He pointed to the ceiling. "Smoke and extreme heat will trigger them. Needless to say, no lighting any joints or cigarettes inside."

"I don't smoke."

"Not many here do. In the case of an emergency, an alarm will sound. You'll be asked to exit your room. Depending on the area of the problem, there are different exits. A series of light strips will activate and show you the way to go."

"If there's power."

Again, he smiled. "You should have been part of our design team. Given the concern about that, the emergency services have two backup power sources. A generator and also solar power run off already full batteries."

"That is good to know." If true. She had a hard time believing someone spent that kind of extra money and time building in multiple failsafes. "Do you have a lot of people working here?" she asked.

To her surprise he gave an exact number. "One hundred and twenty-three at the moment."

Her eyes widened. "That many?"

"A facility such as this requires more staff than you'd think."

Guards, too, given how many she'd noticed thus far. "How many patients does the clinic serve?"

"That varies. Currently we have almost fifty, but that number can go as high as seventy."

Becky bounced into the room. "Nice digs. Where's our stuff so we can unpack?"

"Your luggage will be brought within the next hour while we continue our tour." Lowry led the way back to the elevators and this time he said, "Supply level."

Which was pretty self-explanatory. They didn't actually get their own supplies, but if they had to, there was a guy behind a desk who would dole it out with the proper requisition submitted.

The next level was labs. So many labs with massive viewing windows allowing those who didn't want to suit up and go through the decontamination process to watch.

Levels four and five were the patient levels. Each level was divided into four wings, each wing with eight patient rooms.

Starting in the morning, Margaret would be handling Level Four, Wing B, whereas Becky got assigned Level Four D. At least they wouldn't be working together. Margaret might just put the talkative girl in a coma if she didn't shut up.

"Both wards are under capacity at the moment," Lowry explained as he gave them a peek inside at a few.

"Are they sleeping?" Becky asked, as it seemed every room they glanced in had a prone figure on a bed.

"Sleeping in a sense. This is our coma unit."

"So everyone on this floor is in a coma?" she asked.

"Yes."

"And level five?" she asked.

"Is for recovery."

"So you expect them all to wake up?"

"That is the hope, but..." Lowry shrugged. "Not everyone reacts to treatment the same way."

"What kind of treatment are they getting?" Becky asked.

At the query, Lowry smiled and shook his head. "That part is the secret. We're working on some very advanced medicines and techniques here, which is why we ask for complete confidentiality."

"So long as it's working, it doesn't really matter what you're doing," Margaret murmured. Healing was the most important thing.

"Delighted to hear you say that, Miss Henley. You'll both begin in the morning. Tasks will be noted in the individual patient files." Which were stored on tablets bolted to the foot of their beds.

"What do we do if one of them wakes up?"

Lowry turned a serious gaze on them. "If they so much as twitch, you are to notify us immediately. There is a red button. Press it and vacate the room."

"Shouldn't we stick around in case they wake up with questions?" It would be scary to regain consciousness in a strange place, or so Margaret thought.

"Patients exiting a coma can sometimes exhibit violent outbursts caused by disorientation. We do not want any of our staff injured. We have people trained to handle this."

As a nurse, wasn't Margaret one of those people, though?

Entering the elevator, Lowry said, "And that concludes the tour."

"I thought you said there were six levels." Becky twirled her hair. "What's below us?"

"Another patient level. But there's only one currently being held there, so you won't have to deal with it."

"Wouldn't it make more sense to have that person in one of the empty rooms on levels four and five?" Margaret asked.

"Level six is where we keep those who are a tad more volatile during recovery." Lowry placed his keycard on the pad and was about to speak when the elevator began to move.

"Um, where is it taking us?" Becky asked. "Is it haunted?"

"More like we took too long to give it a destination and someone else called it."

The elevator stopped, and the doors opened, revealing a huge number six on the wall. A man in a white coat with a dark complexion stood waiting and smiled upon seeing them. "Hey Gary. We still on for that beer and watching the game tonight?"

"You bet." Lowry gestured for them to emerge from the elevator. "I'd like you to meet our newest nursing staff additions, Miss Frederickson and Miss Henley. This is Doctor Cerberus."

"The demon dog from Hell. Cool name," Becky blurted out.

"Thank you. I think," the doctor replied, looking somewhat bemused. He appeared about Lowry's age, the silver at his temples aging him despite his smooth mahogany skin.

"Are you done with him for the day?" Lowry asked, glancing at a closed door into Wing A.

"Quite done. He's not cooperating at all. I'd even say it's gotten worse." Cerberus shook his head.

"Shame," Lowry remarked and might have said more except the door behind the doctor opened and a man stuck his head out. "Dr. Cerberus. Thank God you're still here. He's doing something weird."

"Weird how, Shane?" asked the doctor as he grabbed the door and opened it wide, giving them a peek of a long hall with a guard standing in it, talking into a walkie.

Eyes shifted to Margaret and Becky. The young man fidgeted and shoved his glasses firmly on his nose. "You have to see."

"Where is Ivan?" asked Cerberus.

"In the room."

"You left him alone?"

"Sorry. I was trying to make sure I caught you."

"Dammit." Cerberus shoved past the guy, and Lowry stepped forward, his frame keeping the door open. His bulk blocked part of the view, but peeking around his shape, Margaret saw the doctor walking quickly up the hall while the guy who fetched him ran.

Shane slapped his hand by a door and wrenched it open, despite Cerberus yelling, "Stop, you idiot."

But the idiot didn't listen. Shane stood in the open doorway and uttered a questioning, "Ivan?" followed by a squeak as he disappeared suddenly, hauled into the room. There was much crashing, accompanied by the sound of things breaking. The doctor yelled, "Seal the room. Don't let him"—a body flew out and hit the wall—"breach it."

An alarm sounded, and the door in the hall slammed shut. Just in time given something slammed into the portal. Hard.

Lowry barked into the watch on his wrist, "Security to level six."

Something hurtled against the other side of the door again and again. Despite it being made of steel, it dented in more than one spot.

"What is happening?" Margaret asked in a soft whisper, eyes wide.

"Nothing you need to worry about."

Which might have been more reassuring had numerous guards not emerged from the elevator she and Becky had abandoned. They jogged down the hall, their boots a thundering cadence to go with the alarm.

"What are they going to do?" Margaret asked, noticing them pulling the guns by their sides.

"Nothing to worry about, ladies. Tour is over. You can head to your quarters now." Lowry waved them to the elevator, and Becky wasted no time getting in and slapping her card on the reader.

"Habitat level," she said as Lowry continued to watch from the hall.

The banging continued as guards lined up in front of the door, whereas Cerberus stood midway in the hall. She caught of a glimpse of the metal portal buckling and the guards raising their weapons.

Were they seriously going to shoot a patient? The door banged open, and something hurtled into the hall. Something that was hunched and hairy and...snarling?

Then her chance to really grasp what happened disappeared as the elevator doors slid shut.

Becky blew out a breath. "Wow. Am I ever glad we're working with the coma patients."

"I wonder what was wrong with him."

"Probably brain damage. If he was in a coma, then it stands to reason he had head trauma. Could have rattled his mind." Becky swirled a finger by her temple.

"Do you think they shot him?" Margaret gnawed at her lower lip.

She expected Becky to laugh and make light of her comment. To her surprise, the girl took on a serious mien. "I think this place isn't like the hospitals we're used to."

That turned out to be an understatement.

CHAPTER TWO

Luke awoke strapped once more to a medical gurney. He'd yet to get used to it despite it being a common occurrence since saying yes to that prick Chimera all those years ago.

The weight at his wrists let him know he wouldn't be going anywhere. He pulled at the restraints with no result. After his most recent attempt to escape, the tethers were reinforced. All the better to keep him prisoner.

Who knew when Luke agreed to get help he would end up regretting it?

A long sigh heaved from him as he stared at the ceiling. The overhead light was set to dim, enough for those watching to see him. If he could have, he would have flipped them the bird or grabbed his junk and made a kissing noise. Riling his captors was the only enjoyment he got these days. It bugged him to no end that they constantly watched. Took notes. Judged. And mocked.

Mocked his attempts to escape. Made fun of his status.

About the only thing they couldn't make fun of was his cock size. But a big dick was only a prize when it could be used. His had been gathering dust for a while.

He closed his eyes against the dim lighting. How he missed pure dark. The kind that enveloped you like a blanket and hid the ugliness of the world. Such an ugly, ugly world.

In direct contrast, he also missed sunlight. He'd not earned the right to go outside like some of the other patients. Luke wasn't a good boy.

"How many times will it take before you realize we're only trying to help you?" The voice emerged from a speaker, as if Dr. Sphinx would deign to be in the same room. Not since the incident.

"Speaking of help, how is your arm?" Luke broke it when the man thought him unconscious and tried to inject him with some new kind of poison.

"This kind of attitude is why you spend more time asleep than awake," Sphinx chided.

"Ass-kissing was never my forte."

"We simply ask that you respect basic rules."

"How about respecting my right to live free instead of as some kind of guinea pig in your lab?"

"We saved your life."

The clinic had. Yet that didn't mean they owned it.

Especially since the doctors weren't content with just healing. They'd healed him many treatments ago. Now...

Now they were playing God.

"Let me go."

"You know we can't do that. You know too much, Luke. Our fault, we should have been more careful around you." But they weren't. He'd heard everything. Even pretended for a while that he was on their side. Part of their team. Hell, he actually was for a bit until he truly grasped their depravity.

"I won't tell anyone about your illegal experiments." Who would believe him? And if he showed them proof? He'd end up strapped to another bed. Or dead with a bullet in his brain.

"You can't leave. Not yet. You're not ready. And we're within our rights to keep you until we deem you fit for society. You signed the papers."

Because Chimera had fooled him. "I never agreed to this." He strained at the straps. Never agreed to a prisoner for years with his only crime wanting to be whole again.

"If you controlled your temper—"

Luke roared, the sound more beast than man. "I didn't have a problem with my temper until you made me a monster." Not entirely true, then again, the truth wasn't something they cared about much around here.

"You will remain restrained until we trust that you can behave yourself."

That day would never come. Especially since he

couldn't fake it. Luke hated Sphinx with a passion. The so-called doctor thought himself above laws and played God with people's lives.

Some days Luke wondered if he'd have been better dying that day in the desert or resigning himself to a life in a wheelchair. At least then he would have his freedom—and pizza. How he fucking missed pizza.

"One day I will kill you." It was the one thing that kept him going.

"More like one day you will get on your knees to thank me for making you better than you were."

Highly unlikely. "So what's on the agenda today? Gonna suck me dry of blood? Stick needles in my bones?" To draw out his marrow. "Is it hamster tread-mill day?" As they tested his stamina and monitored his vitals.

"Given your escapade yesterday? Today you get to do nothing. Same tomorrow. As a matter of fact, I don't foresee needing you the rest of this week. Enjoy the bed rest."

The asshole planned to leave him tied to the bed for a week?

The very idea slipped past his nonchalant shield. "You can't do this."

"I can and will. Enjoy the break. I know I will."

"Let me go." He strained against his tethers.

"No. I think it's time you understood what it means to truly be a prisoner. With no freedom at all. I've been nice up to now. But you..." Dr. Sphinx sighed. "You just can't behave yourself. So let this be a lesson that your life can be much, much worse."

"Asshole. You can't do this," Luke yelled. "I'll tell Chimera you're mistreating his star patient."

"Chimera won't do a thing. And neither will your precious Dr. Cerberus. He's gone, for a few weeks at least. Off securing investors and wowing them with our progress."

Not good news. At least Cerberus respected the lives of his patients. To Sphinx, Luke and the others like him were just test subjects. He really didn't care if they lived or died. Or in this case went insane.

"You can't leave me tied up." The panic in him built. A beast inside his chest, pushing to get out.

"I can. I will. Think about your behavior. It doesn't have to be like this."

"Bastard," he yelled. He struggled, but it changed nothing. Sphinx kept his word. No one came to release him.

Not that day.

Or the next.

As time passed, hour upon hour, he began to struggle in earnest. Yanking at the straps, cursing, foaming. The rage filling him with bloody thoughts.

The primal need to escape filled him, and he bucked as he roared. And kept roaring, hearing the satisfying sound of metal bending.

Yes. Just a little more. The adrenaline made him strong. The bars on his bed groaned louder.

The hiss of gas couldn't be ignored, and his lungs

filled with the noxious cloud. The drug knocked him out. He awoke strapped to a new bed with even tougher restraints he discovered as he fought to free himself.

The cycle repeated itself, with the only change being the IVs in his body feeding him, draining waste. Making him into nothing.

Less than nothing.

He felt even more invalid now than after his injury.

Which was why he stopped fighting. Stopped everything.

Caring.

Surviving.

He let his body shut down.

Let it end.

Set me free.

CHAPTER THREE

Almost a month here and Margaret was no closer to figuring this place out. While Chimaeram made a specific request to hire nurses, she soon realized they could have employed just about anybody, given she'd not done anything truly medical thus far apart from drawing blood and oral swabs.

The ward she'd been assigned contained eight rooms but only six patients. All in a coma. Four men and two women. Her job? Drawing blood once in the morning then again at night. Ensuring their feeding tubes remained unclogged, their hydrating saline drips remained full. Massaging their bodies to keep their muscles from atrophying. And flipping them to prevent bedsores.

Then there was the less pleasant aspect of changing their bodily waste bags. Bathing them done with an averted gaze because it felt wrong to denude someone and wash them without permission.

Given their comatose state, she had difficulty understanding why these men and women were kept in separate rooms instead of a ward. It would have made more sense. Then there was the question of, how did their families visit them? In all the time she'd been here, not one had received a visitor. It seemed odd to say the least.

Also odd was the cause of the deep sleep. The patient files she was given access to didn't mention any accidents or give a viral excuse—nor did it provide names, instead assigning the patients identification numbers. How impersonal.

While a few in her care had the lingering remains of scarring from an injury, two of them didn't have any kind of marks. So why did they sleep?

Was it even a natural slumber?

These questions led to her wonder what was in the third IV. The one she wasn't supposed to touch. Yet it intrigued her, especially given the liquid in the clear tube and bag changed color from room to room. A pale glowing green for Patient RP351. Pink for the female patient SC129. Two variations of blue for the next two guys, red for the fourth fellow, and then a black fluid for the last woman.

What kind of medicine did these patients receive? Was it even legal?

She wondered and yet didn't dare ask. Her contract specifically stated no discussing her employment or what she saw, not even with other staff.

Becky didn't let the warning deter her. When she

joined Margaret outside for one of their rare matching breaks, she tried to talk shop. "I lost one of my patients overnight."

"I'm sorry. That must be hard."

The other woman waved a hand. "I don't mean he died, silly. At least I don't think he did. But JR"—the name she'd assigned the big, burly dude with short-cropped hair—"was gone when I went in this morning."

"Perhaps he recovered and was moved to another wing."

Becky shrugged. "Could be. Although I asked some of the nurses on level five and they said they hadn't gotten anyone new."

"Then maybe he was on the helicopter that left last night." Margaret really wished Becky would stop talking about it. It wasn't any of their business. She'd signed a contract. She had the balance with four zeroes in her bank account to protect.

"Maybe he left. It is super weird, though. You'd think they'd put him in recovery. You know, to make sure he doesn't lapse."

"I didn't think coma patients lapsed."

Becky shrugged. "No idea. These are my first. You haven't lost any of yours yet, have you?"

Margaret shook her head. "Nope." Not a twitch from any of them. At times it felt like she cared for corpses.

"Janey says they've been prepping her two empty rooms. She thinks she's getting some new ones."

From where? How did Chimaeram select its patients? "I think it's good they're filling the empty beds. I can tell you right now, most coma wards don't get the personalized care these guys get."

"True, but still, I've got to wonder." Becky leaned close and whispered in a voice that nonetheless carried, "What do you think they're pumping them with?"

Rather than speculate, Margaret shrugged. "None of my business."

"I think it's experimental shit."

Margaret thought so, too, but she ate her sandwich rather than agree.

"And I don't think their comas were caused by an accident."

"Some were." No denying patient DG41 bore scars, some on his face and many more on his body. Although those scars had faded since her arrival. Perhaps the fluid in the IV acted as a super-healing agent.

"Yeah, I'll give you a couple look like they did a few rounds with a meat grinder, but Pixie Girl, she is like perfect. Not a single mark on her. I swear, she's like a sleeping beauty waiting for true love's kiss." Becky puckered up and made smooching noises.

"Don't do it."

"I won't. I'm not that desperate." Becky rolled her eyes. "But she is hot."

"I should get back to work." Margaret gathered her things.

"I'm going to pop in and check on Larry. He was

sweating earlier. Then I want to grab a nap before my next shift starts." She wrinkled her nose. "Still don't get why they need so much care. It's not like they're going anywhere."

Margaret didn't understand either, but the job was easy enough, if boring. Becky waved as she skipped off. Margaret spent the fifteen minutes she had left face turned to the sun. She wasn't in any hurry to return underground.

Eventually her break ended, and she had to go back to work. She disposed of her trash on her way back in and made her way to level four, her key card giving her access through the various locked doors until she reached the one for her ward. A press of her card against the reader didn't activate the lock. She tugged on the handle anyhow. The door refused to open. She frowned.

Slapped the card again. And again. When it continued to refuse to work, she pressed a button beside a speaker.

The intercom hissed with static. "State your name and issue."

"Hi, this is Nurse Henley. My card's not working. I can't get into my ward."

"One moment please." The static cut off, and she waited as he checked on his end. This had happened once before. The magnetic stripe on her card failed, a problem which was easily fixed.

The speaker crackled. "Ward Four, all sections are off-limits until further notice."

"Why?"

"That's classified."

Classified? What kind of answer was that? "Have I been reassigned elsewhere?" Or was she being sent home? That would suck. The job might bore her to tears, but it paid really well.

"Hold on while I check."

It took several minutes before the voice returned. "You're being assigned a new patient. Level six. Ward B, room six oh two."

Level six? That was where the patient supposedly woke up and went crazy. Crazy enough to smash open a door.

Fear dried her mouth, but curiosity found the words needed. "When do I start?"

"Now."

She wondered if the other nurses on this floor, including Becky, had been reassigned elsewhere. Taking the elevator down, she felt some trepidation as it jolted to a stop and the doors slid open. The last time she'd been here, someone had gone nuts. Nuts enough the guards that usually just stood around had gathered.

With guns.

The reminder she didn't hear them fire only partially reassured. Would she have to worry about another patient going crazy? Was it an isolated instance? Lowry himself said level six was for the more dangerous elements.

Kind of scary. However, dealing with erratic patients wasn't a new thing for her. Time in the ER had brought in more than a few people spaced out on drugs. And if things got a little out of control...then she would scream loud enough to bring some guards.

Her pep talk only partially worked. Exiting the elevator, she was faced with a few locked doors. The B Ward was to her left, not straight ahead where the crazy guy was kept.

The key card worked on the access pad, and the heavy door opened. The hallway only had two doors, and want to guess which one had the guard stationed outside it?

She paused, staring at the number painted on the concrete wall.

"Ma'am, can I help you?" The guard put his hand on his weapon and positioned himself in front of the door.

"I was told to come to room six oh two and provide care for the patient inside."

"Card please." He held out his hand, and she unclipped it from her white blouse, handing it to him.

He scanned it against a portable tablet and perused the screen before handing it back. "You are cleared to proceed. If the patient shows any signs of movement, please exit the room immediately."

Not exactly the most reassuring thing to hear. "Is he sleeping?"

"I'm not at liberty to discuss that, ma'am."

She turned before rolling her eyes. Idiot. As if telling her whether the guy was awake or not was some kind of secret. She placed her card against the access panel. The snick of the lock disengaging, numerous locks she might add, didn't help the trepidation.

The soldier held himself across from the door, tense, hand still on his gun.

Really, really not reassuring.

Still, she'd not heard of any of the nurses being injured since her arrival. Two had left, but that was normal given they were only here on limited time contracts.

Holding on to her fear, she entered the room. The dimly lit room. Different than the coma patient rooms on Ward Four where the lights remained on at all times.

She reached for the dimmer switch by the door, increasing the brightness until she could see. Plain gray walls made of almost seamless concrete, unlike the plaster on the other levels. Equipment lined them, some with blinking lights, all of them humming. The floor was more concrete with a drain to the side. Strange since she'd not seen the like elsewhere. Then again, as the lowermost floor, perhaps it was necessary for flooding issues.

Not exactly a great thought to have so far underground.

While the concrete space proved different, there were similarities to her previous ward. The IV poles standing in a corner, unused. Only a pair. The third that usually hung with a colored bag of fluid appeared to be missing.

She took in all those details before looking at the patient himself, a rather large man strapped to a bed.

Approaching, she took note of his handsome appearance. Hair a golden brown and thick. His face bearing stubble. His lashes long and hitting his cheeks as he slept.

Unlike the patients upstairs, there were no IVs marring the skin of his arms. Not even one for hydration. Obviously not in a coma, which explained the guard outside. Was he the same one who went crazy the day she arrived?

Did it matter? A patient was a patient.

She cleared her throat. "Excuse me."

No movement.

She placed her hand on his skin, felt the feverish heat of it and recoiled.

Not a single change in the cadence of his breathing. Yet...every hair on her body lifted.

She reached out again and shook his arm. "Excuse me, I don't mean to wake you, but I'm here to take some vitals."

While there was no reply, she could have sworn he listened. Which was crazy. Why would he fake sleep? And why did she see cuffs around his wrists?

She noted the metal link going over both wrists. A flip of the sheet by his feet showed his ankles similarly tethered.

Very curious. While restraints were sometimes used in hospitals, it was only as a last resort.

"What did you do to deserve this?" she murmured aloud.

She moved to the tablet inset on the foot of his bed. A tap of the screen drew up the basics. His name was missing, no surprise. The ID given was WF007. Like the other charts, it didn't list any medical condition. No treatment. Nothing. Just instructions on his care.

First item on the list: drawing samples. Easy enough. She rolled over a trolley tray with all the needed items ready for her use. The only problem was the empty box of gloves.

A search of the cabinets didn't reveal any other boxes. She eyed the door. Would the guard fetch her some if she asked?

She poked her head out the door and stared wide eyed at the gun pointing at her face. "Eep."

"Sorry, ma'am. You're supposed to give warning before exiting the room."

"I didn't know that. I'll remember for next time." Because she didn't want to soil herself by accident if the trigger-happy guard did it again.

"Are you done?" he asked.

"No. I need gloves. Can I grab some from another room?"

"Sorry, ma'am. You're only authorized for entry into this one."

"Can you get me some?"

"I am not allowed to leave my post."

She held in a sigh. "Then what are you allowed to do? I'm supposed to wear them."

"I will put in a call and see if Supply can send some down."

Which was obviously the best she was going to get.

Returning to the room, she eyed her patient's prone body. She didn't really need gloves to draw blood. So long as she didn't get any of his blood in an open wound, she would avoid contamination. Since her hands were injury free, she quickly set the tourniquet over his upper arm, noticing the thick muscle. Thicker than expected given his coma.

Perhaps he was more recently afflicted, and his muscles hadn't had time to atrophy.

The blood filled the tubes, a dark red, thick and sluggish. She unwound the rubber band around his arm and got her quota. When she withdrew the needle, she had the cotton ball ready. But he didn't bleed. She couldn't even see the hole the needle left behind.

"Guess you don't need a Band-Aid." She left his side and placed the vials of blood in a refrigerated compartment on the wall. The moment the door closed, she heard a whirring sound. Curious, she pulled at the door and gaped at the empty spot where she'd put the samples.

"Well, that saves running them around to the lab," she muttered.

Next on her list, blood pressure, which was low, probably on account he slept. Listening to his heart, which beat strong and slow, she noted all the numbers on the tablet, entering them in along with the time.

With all the vitals handled, it was time to bathe

him. She prepared a warm basin of water and grabbed a cloth from the cupboard. She hesitated beside it because she'd yet to receive the gloves she'd asked for.

Would someone be arriving with them soon? Should she ask the guard again?

Or should she just get the bathing over with? Bathing and a massage were the last things she needed to do before punching out.

It wouldn't kill her to use her bare hands. The patient obviously didn't have anything contagious, or she wouldn't be allowed in the room.

Still, there was something intimate about taking a damp cloth and running it over his bare skin. The facecloth covering her hand should have been a barrier, and yet she was acutely aware of him. Aware of his body. His very attractive body.

She averted her gaze and washed blind, running the cloth over the many ridges of his stomach. Rinsed it and then started again on a new section. With his upper body clean, she had to start on the lower half. She placed the sheet over his torso so that he wouldn't catch a chill and then commenced on his legs. Moved up to the thighs.

Last, the groin. She averted her gaze as she moved the sheet high enough for her to wash him. She swirled the cloth around his penis, a penis that was rather sizeable,, she noted, despite it being dormant. She scrubbed over his sac and, in the process, ended up with his shaft flopping onto her hand.

Direct skin contact. With a strange, sleeping man's penis! But that wasn't the worst part.

It can't be...

She glanced over to see his shaft inflating, getting bigger and bigger. Her eyes got wider in equal measure.

But it was the, "Go ahead and touch it again," that had her squeaking.

"You're awake!"

CHAPTER FOUR

Luke had actually been awake for a while, but feigned sleep. No point in letting the doctors know he was metabolizing the drugs quicker than expected. Fuckers would increase his dose, otherwise.

From the moment the nurse entered, he'd discerned she was new. Easily noticeable in the hesitation in her movements, a gentleness that wasn't present with those who'd been around for a while.

He'd hoped she would ignore instructions and undo one of his restraints, but she did her job without even loosening them. A shame. Not that one free arm would help him much. His last attempt to escape he'd only made it to the hall before the tranquilizer darts dropped him.

The good news was the drugs took longer to act. That was the problem when you used them too often; the body got used to them. He'd managed to take down a few of the guards before they pumped enough of the stuff into his veins to make him face plant.

He'd yet to see himself in a mirror and catalogue the damage to his nose. He remembered hearing it crunch as he fell. He could breathe just fine, though. Perhaps they'd set it while he was out. Not that the doctors cared how he looked. Luke was no longer their poster boy for what the treatment could do.

Once upon a time he would have shouted their praises from the mountaintops. Now he wanted to paint the snow on those peaks with their blood.

Did they know just how violent his thoughts had become? Was this why they sent fresh meat to care for him? Send in the lamb to see if he would slaughter.

Or did they really not realize he was awake? Possible because Luke faked sleep well. Modulating his heart rate, his breathing. Even managing to not flinch when a penlight was shone in his eyes.

Usually he ignored those puttering around him. However, something about the new nurse drew him. Intrigued him.

She smelled nice. Very nice. Certainly nicer than those fucking doctors. Especially Sphinx who always had to have a cigarette before coming to see him. Gag me with a spoon. He hated fucking stale nicotine smoke.

Sphinx would be the only one he wouldn't take a bite of when he escaped. He'd never get the taste off his tongue. With that asshole, he'd use his bare hands.

Squeeze the life out of him. Watch as his eyes went blank.

Goals.

Goals he'd given up on since his decision to let it all go.

If only that didn't feel like the cowardly route. Giving up wasn't easy. He wanted to fight. He had been fighting, but eventually Luke had to admit there was no escape. No way out of this nightmare he'd signed up for.

"Sorry if this is cold."

What? He almost opened his eyes to ask her what she meant, only to feel the wet swipe of a cloth by his neck where it met his shoulder. It slid down his arm, in between his fingers, then disappeared. He heard the slosh of water as she rinsed the cloth then tackled the other shoulder and arm.

Usually being helpless and washed like a child bothered him. More than one nurse had gotten growled at and scared off. But there was a certain sensuality to having her do it. The slow drag of cloth over skin, the fleeting touch of her flesh.

A touch that affected him more than it should have.

He controlled himself, though, even as each stroke of the wet cloth titillated. However, he wasn't about to get a boner for a woman who could be a hundred years old for all he knew.

Except, he had a feeling she was young. Not super young, but nubile enough to make a man have thoughts. Thoughts that would lead nowhere. When was the last time he'd had sex?

Certainly not since he'd been taken prisoner—the second time. Once he caught on to what was happening, he'd rebelled and lost all privileges, including that of pussy.

He'd lost track of how many days, weeks, months, or was it now years since that happened. Couldn't even remember the last time he jacked one off. The funny part was the doctors in this place asked for samples. More like demanded. Even offered him a woman if he didn't want to use his hand.

He wasn't about to give them anything, especially not his seed. The fact they might have milked him while he slept bothered. He could only hope the act of taking it by medical means rendered it useless.

Which made him wonder, was this part of a new plan? Send in a fresh nurse, one with a gentle touch. Who smelled good. Who conveniently had no gloves to use.

It shouldn't have mattered. He'd been touched and prodded so much that he'd learned to control every reaction. It was the only way to defy them.

Yet, his control failed him today. Her bare skin touching him ignited his blood, and when her flesh came in contact with his cock? His body reacted. He got hard. He got vulgar. Touch me again, indeed. No wonder the nurse with her perky little cap eyed him as if he'd said something dirty. Because he totally had.

And now that he'd seen her, he kind of wished

she'd come back over with that cloth and continue. She was young. Late twenties, maybe early thirties, with a trim figure, clear skin, and dark hair pulled back from her face. She wore the usual company uniform consisting of a white blouse, dark slacks, and a white cap on her head replete with a red cross. A strange uniform choice that served no real purpose, and yet all the nurses wore them.

Just like all the guards wore black combat outfits and carried guns.

It made him wonder why the villains in charge of the operation didn't sport little mustaches that they twirled when making up their devious plots. Alas, the bad guys in his life story were clean cut, intelligent, and well dressed, which, in some respects, made it worse.

"You're awake," she repeated, still staring at him with the biggest brownest eyes.

"Your power of observation is astounding," was his sarcastic reply.

"How long have you been awake?"

"Awhile."

"Why didn't you say anything?"

"Didn't want to miss the show. Don't mind me. Go ahead and finish the job." He jerked his hips—the only thing he could move—this time being intentionally crude in the hopes she'd leave and his body could calm down. Because his erection wasn't getting any smaller. On the contrary, the more he inhaled her scent, the more he looked upon her, the hornier he got.

Rather than stomp off, railing about sexual harassment, she slapped him with the washcloth.

A wet cloth snapped onto his dick and balls.

He might have let out an unmanly yodel. "Jeezus, lady, what the fuck?"

"I thought you wanted me touching you," she said a tad too sweetly. "Too rough? So sorry. Now that I'm done cleaning your ball sac, let me finish by wiping your face." She brought the cloth close to his mouth, and he yelled.

"Don't you fucking dare."

"Or what? According to my epic powers of observation you're in no position to do a damned thing."

He glared. "You're mean." And adorable at the same time given she didn't cower. If she only knew who she teased. What he was capable of. She'd run screaming from the room.

"I'm mean?" she choked the query out. "You're the one asking for a hand job. I'm a nurse, not a prostitute."

"Sexual healing is as important as the rest." He just couldn't seem to stop.

"Abstinence strengthens the body for healing. Obviously, you need to regain your strength, or you wouldn't be here."

"I'm here because of some sick fuck—"

"Nurse Henley," a speaker crackled. "Your duties are done for the day. Please exit the room."

"What the heck?" She stared at the ceiling. "Is someone watching?"

"They're always watching," Luke muttered.

"I wasn't quite done with the patient." Spoken aloud even as she walked over to the sink to rinse her hands.

The disembodied voice replied, "Someone else will see to the patient. Please exit the room and proceed to the first level. You are to see Doctor Chimera in his office."

"How's it going, Sphincter?" Luke deliberately mispronounced the name. One of his many ways to needle the doctor who spied yet again.

"Ready for your next nap already? That can be arranged," was the ominous threat.

The nurse caught the exchange and frowned as she dried her hands. "Are you sure—"

Sphinx cut her off. "Now, Miss Henley." The microphone cut out, and yet Luke knew someone still listened. They always listened.

He wanted to tell her, *Don't go.* Having her near was a pleasure he didn't understand. It also posed a danger. "Listen, you seem like a nice lady. So I'm going to give you a friendly piece of advice. You need to go. Run. As far and fast away from this place as you can."

"Why?"

He sealed his lips. Was it fair to burden this woman with the secrets he knew? Secrets that might kill her?

"Just trust me when I say you need to get out of here." Before it was too late.

The door opened, and the guard stepped inside. "Ma'am, I have orders to ensure you vacate the room."

The guard's hand sat on the grip of his weapon. So afraid, even though Luke was all tied up. It brought a smile to his lips.

Nice to know my reputation lingers.

She noticed the wariness in the guard and yet didn't run from the room. Brave and foolish all at once.

"A second, please, while I toss this out." She turned and took the paper towel she'd used to dry her hands to the waste receptacle, the stiff silence in the room fraught with restrained violence. And not just from the guard.

He didn't like the way the fellow eyed her then smirked at Luke. His lip curled into a snarl that practically dared the guy.

The nurse didn't glance at him, not once as she scurried from the room.

Good riddance.

He didn't need the complication.

Problem was he forgot nothing he ever did was unseen. Every move he made. Every word he spoke... Every erection. Catalogued.

Sphinx returned to chat the moment the door slammed shut. "I see you've been fooling us with your extended naps. It must be time to increase your dose again."

"Suck my dick." The mature thing to say when a prisoner of mad scientists.

"Me? Wouldn't you rather Nurse Henley put her lips on you? You showed quite the interest in her."

He inadvertently had and now pretended it meant nothing. "She's a woman. I'm a man. It happens."

"It's never happened before."

True, and Luke still didn't understand why it happened now. "I got a boner. Big fucking deal."

"It is as a matter of fact."

"Won't happen again. I can promise you that." The nurse took him by surprise. He'd be better prepared next time. If there was a next time. He found it interesting the way they yanked her so quickly. And sending her to Chimera? Had she done something she shouldn't have?

Like wake the sleeping beast...

"You still haven't learned, have you?" The doctor's voice dropped low. "We are giving you a chance here, a chance to become something bigger and better."

"I'm your guinea pig and prisoner. What does being agreeable get me? More needles? Gee, sign me the fuck up."

"Those who toe the line get privileges."

"You mean those who shove their nose up your ass get to go outside on a leash." He sneered. "Been there. Done that." And those small tastes of freedom proved even more cruel than the restraints.

"The leash is for those who still have an urge to run. If you would prove yourself loyal—"

"Won't happen, asshole. Chimera lied to me. You used me. Abused me. And now you want me to agree to more of your bullshit? I'd rather die." Luke thought about it. A lot. What was the point of living?

A pair of glinting eyes and sassy lips suddenly came to mind.

He closed his mind against them. There was no hope for him. No chance even if he broke these chains. Sphinx and his doctor pals had made sure of that. He could never have a normal life.

Never be with a woman. Would never dare.

Which was why he wanted to die. Why he'd willed his body to reject everything they tried to inject him with. Drugs. Food. Water. His body said no to them all.

Despite his intrigue with the nurse, he wouldn't be swayed from his course. He took charge of the only thing he could control.

His demise.

Sphinx uttered a disdainful chuckle. "Die? Such melodrama. You won't die. We won't let you."

"Let?" Luke snorted. "You don't control me."

"Yet. We've just got to find the right combination. Now say good night, Luke. I'm tripling your dose."

For once, he didn't want to sleep. Didn't want to succumb. He needed to stay awake to stop them from doing things that kept him alive.

Closing his eyes, he drew from deep within and struggled. Roared. Bucked. Rampaged like a beast, to no avail. The hiss of gas filled the room, and sweet oblivion took him.

CHAPTER FIVE

THE GUARD DIDN'T LEAVE MARGARET'S SIDE UNTIL he'd seen her to the elevator. Even then, he told the computer which floor and waited for the doors to close.

Such caution in escorting her away from the man in 602. Who was he? Certainly not a coma patient. Nor did she see any sign of injury. So why did the clinic have him? The restraints obviously meant they thought him dangerous. To himself or others?

With his sarcastic manner, she tended to think the latter. He had too much arrogance to harm himself.

Which again begged the question, what were they treating him for? While she'd bathed him, she'd not paid close attention to his body, but the parts she'd seen appeared unblemished. Perfect.

Sexy.

Such an inappropriate thought to have about a patient. Especially one with problems.

What was wrong with him? Doubtful she'd find

out. Getting called into Doctor Chimera's office—the man who'd founded the Chimaeram clinic—couldn't bode well. Given she'd never met him, she wondered if she was about to get fired, which was totally unfair. She'd not done anything wrong. Mostly.

I did intentionally snap him with the damp cloth.

Then again, the patient started it with his rudeness. Asking her to take care of his erection. He totally deserved what he got.

However, her actions might have crossed a line. She should have walked away rather than let her temper get the best of her. What did it say about her that she abused a man who couldn't protect himself?

She'd soon find out. Obviously, someone watching reported her actions, and now she'd probably be told to leave. The very idea made her stomach sink. She'd never been reprimanded before, let alone fired.

The elevator stopped at the first floor above ground, spilling her into the long hallway that Margaret used to think went nowhere. Wrong.

The doors to the offices of those highly positioned in the clinic were simply well hidden, blending seamlessly into the wall. She wouldn't have even known where to go if the opening hadn't suddenly appeared, a section of the wall sliding into a recess, startling her.

She peeked inside and noticed an antechamber with polished wood floors, pale blue walls, a small window showing the slanting late afternoon daylight, and a desk behind which sat an older woman.

"Um, hello. I'm looking for Dr. Chimera's office?"

The woman raised her gaze, stern behind glasses perched low on her nose. "Sit. He'll be with you in a moment." The head then ducked again and continued to peruse a computer screen while fingers tapped at a keyboard.

Feeling like a rebuked child, she dropped into a chair. Hands tucked in her lap, Margaret glanced around the sterile space, which lacked wall décor of any kind. It could use a splash of color. Even elevator music would have done something to improve the ambiance of the place.

Then again, when being called in, probably for a dress-down, one shouldn't get too comfortable.

After what seemed an interminable moment, the secretary lifted her head and said, "You may go in."

Having never met the elusive Dr. Chimera—because the doctors had their living quarters on the second floor of the above-ground structure—Margaret had nonetheless formed an image in her mind. An older gent, probably short and balding, a real scientific type, who preferred books to the outdoors.

She couldn't have been more wrong.

First off, Dr. Chimera was young, thirties, maybe forties at the most. Tall too, well over six feet, with dark hair swept back from his brow and piercing blue eyes. He filled out his casual polo shirt well, his tanned arms muscled, his hands large.

His smile stretched wide and welcoming. "Nurse Henley, sorry to keep you waiting. I was dealing with a patient issue. Please, have a seat."

She perched on the edge of the club chair facing his desk and was treated to a panorama of the mountains at his back. The perks of being in charge.

"You wished to speak with me, sir."

"I did. I hear you've been doing excellent work."

She almost blurted out, "You have?" but managed instead to reply, "Thank you, sir."

"I trust you're enjoying your employment with us."

"Yes." She stuck to simple answers.

"Excellent. We value those who work for us, which is why I wanted to personally apologize for the crassness of your last patient."

"You do?" Her surprise appeared in her query.

"He is quite vulgar. But you handled yourself very well."

She blinked and like an idiot said, "I slapped him in his man parts with a washcloth."

"Which he deserved." She was treated to a Colgate-white smile. "You are obviously a woman who knows how to handle someone difficult like Luke."

Luke? The man had a name. She had begun to wonder if any of the patients did. "What's wrong with him?"

"War wounds. A bullet shattered his hip. Another pierced his spleen. He almost lost his arm. He spilled a lot of blood before the medics got to him and went into cardiac arrest during transport a few times. He's technically died twice."

"He seemed rather alive to me."

"The miracle of medicine," Chimera said with a

smile. "However, I'm afraid his injuries left him a tad damaged up here." He tapped at his temple.

"Is that why he's in restraints?"

"He's proven unfortunately violent since his recovery. But here at Chimaeram, we specialize in difficult cases. We are working on a solution for his violent outbursts."

"How?" she couldn't help asking.

"I'm afraid that part of it is confidential. Can't be giving away our trade secrets." Dr. Chimera winked. "However, rest assured we are working on some cutting-edge treatments. Things that will revolutionize medical care for everyone."

"That sounds great."

"It is, but I didn't call you here to give you a sales pitch. Given how well you acquitted yourself, I'd like you to take on Luke as your primary patient."

"I don't understand." She truly didn't. She'd come here expecting a dressing-down or even firing.

"I mean I'd like you to care for him exclusively. I'm afraid he's intimidated the others on staff. But I think you're made of sterner stuff."

"Sure. I mean I'm here to do whatever the company needs." So long as those checks kept coming. "What would I have to do?"

"On top of the things you've done today, we'd also like you to take care of his feeding, since he doesn't thrive on intravenous. Bathing, of course. We'll let you know what samples we require and when."

"Will he be restrained at all times?"

"Yes. He really shouldn't be let loose. For your safety. We wouldn't want anything to happen to you." Said with another smile and yet she sensed a strange undercurrent.

"It could be some of his outbursts are because of the fact he's tied down."

"I'm sure you're right, and I wish we didn't have to use them. Perhaps you can help us get him to a place where he realizes we're here to help. Not harm."

"I'm not a psychiatrist."

"No, but you have compassion tempered with steel." Chimera leaned forward. "He spoke to you, which is more than he's done with previous nurses."

Which would be flattering if... "I hardly think asking for sexual favors is a conversation."

"He also told you to flee, did he not?" Chimera remarked, proving he had listened or someone had informed him.

"Yeah. He said to run as far and fast as I could. He didn't say why."

The doctor waved a hand. "The why is obvious. He thinks he can protect you."

"From who?"

"The big bad doctors." He winked. "He's yet to realize we're not the enemy. But given he's shown an interest in you, perhaps he'll listen."

"I'm a stranger."

"For now. As his full-time nurse, you'll be able to develop a bond with him. Form some trust. Make him realize that by working with us, he is working for himself."

The fact that his man hadn't given up on his patient fired something in her, reminded her of the reason she'd gotten into nursing in the first place. "When do I start?"

"First thing in the morning. Say eight a.m. until eleven. Then resuming at one until three. Then a quick evening shift at six until eight to give him his supper and prepare him for bed."

Seven hours split. Not bad. "Sounds good, sir."

"No need to be so formal. We're colleagues. Call me Adrian."

He already probably knew but she said, "Margaret."

"Lovely name for a lovely lady. It was a pleasure to meet you."

"And you, sir."

"Good luck with your new duties, and if you have any concerns about Luke, don't hesitate to come see me."

She left his office somewhat bemused. To have gone in expecting a scolding and come out with what almost felt like a promotion. Odd.

She made her way to her quarters, wondering about her new patient. Curious about Dr. Chimera—because how did a man that young get put in charge of what was obviously a big and expensive project?

The cafeteria was serving dinner, and she grabbed a tray of food, choosing one of the single tables despite the invitation by some guards to join them. She wasn't quite at the point yet where she wanted to get involved with anyone. It proved a quiet dinner given Becky didn't join her.

Speaking of whom, she noted Becky's door was closed as she made her way to her room. Usually the talkative nurse kept it open when she was off shift, blasting music or chatting anyone up on their way through the hall. Not that she had many people to accost for conversation. The wing was for females only, and not only were many of the rooms lacking occupants, a good number of the women were rather standoffish, like Adrian's secretary. Margaret had only rarely seen her in the halls and never at the cafeteria.

With the hour still being early, she spent a moment on the computer in her room using the internet. She knew everything she did online was monitored; however, she didn't see anything wrong with checking out her boss.

She'd just met him, making her curiosity normal. Typing in "Doctor Chimera" didn't get her any hits, not real ones at any rate. Lots of listings about mythical monsters and science involving the hybrid splicing of genes.

Crazy stuff that was thankfully only a theory. Science fiction novels made it seem feasible. The mix of man and animal. Good thing humanity knew better than to play God.

Since her search proved too vague, she did more searches, all of them leading to more dead ends and a disturbing image on one website of a dog spliced with a cat. Not as cute as you'd expect and obviously Photoshopped.

She idly typed in the word Luke.

That proved useless with a gazillion hits.

Then Luke injury. Luke shattered hip.

Nothing. No surprise. Without a last name it was worse than finding the very tiny tip of a needle in a haystack.

Shutting down the computer, she went to bed, but lay awake. Thinking of her new patient.

Which might be why, when she fell asleep, she dreamt of him.

She was in a field. Lush and green. The grass verdant and soft, tickling her bare feet. She glanced down at her toes. Wiggled them. How real it felt. Real and yet surreal given no grass ever looked so perfect, each strand the same height. The green hue uniform. When she brushed it with her toes, the stalks immediately returned to a standing position.

"Softer than any carpet." The deep rumble drew her gaze ahead of her, and she blinked.

Gaped, as well, for Luke stood in the field. Nude. And looking mighty fine.

Margaret eyed him, the width of his shoulders, the toned strength of his arms, the ridge of his abs, the vee...

She averted her gaze. "You're naked."

"So are you."

At his reply, she glanced down and squeaked,

threw her hands over the obvious bits, but that did little to hide the goodies. Her cheeks heated, and he chuckled. "Why hide it, Florence?"

"My name isn't Florence."

He shrugged, a roll of those big bare shoulders that caused moist heat to blossom between her legs. "You look like a Florence Nightingale, especially in that hot cap." He gave a jerk of his head.

She didn't dare let go of her cooch or her boobs, but a bob of her head showed the damned hat perched on her head. She sighed. "It is the most ridiculous thing."

"I think it's cute."

"Said by a man who doesn't deal with bobby pins every morning. Any idea where I am?"

"In a field."

She cast him a glare. "Duh. I see that. I just don't recognize it."

He looked around. "Probably because it isn't a real place but a construct."

Construct as in a dream. "I wonder why a field, though." And where were her clothes? She'd given up on hiding her body. Stupid to be embarrassed considering none of this was real.

"Makes sense to me. Field of dreams."

"That's the title of a movie."

"It started out as a quote first."

"I can't believe I'm arguing with you." He wasn't real. "This is crazy." She shook her head.

"Here I would have called it the most fun I've had in a while. Usually when those fucktards drug me, I sink into a black hole. You're an unexpected treat."

She snickered. "Oh, that's priceless. Dream-you thinks he's dreaming me. Sorry to break it to you, but this is my subconscious screwing around."

"Oh really?" The hint of a smile hovered on his lips. "And why exactly would your subconscious be dreaming of me?"

Her turn to shrug. "Because you're hot, and I haven't had sex in a bit."

"So you want to screw me? I'm game."

Her cheeks flamed as dream Luke spread his arms wide in invitation. "I do not want to screw you."

"Are you sure? Because I'm totally willing."

"I would never sleep with a patient."

"But you said it yourself, this is a dream."

A dream that felt real and she probably wouldn't remember when she woke. "I don't know you."

"Is that a prerequisite for good sex?" He stepped closer, and she could have sworn she felt heat radiating off of him, scorching her skin.

"This is nuts."

"Totally." His hand cupped the back of her head, fingers threading through her hair, drawing her near.

"I don't kiss strangers."

"How can I be a stranger when I've seen you naked?" he whispered against her lips.

She closed her eyes as his mouth slanted over hers. Her breath caught at the soft sensuality of the kiss. A kiss that ignited a fire.

Their naked bodies touched, and while it wasn't the same electric shock as in person, she leaned into the warmth of him, the sleek smoothness and hardness of his body. The hair on his chest, thick and golden, tickled. His free hand curled around her waist and pulled her close. Close enough his erection became trapped between them.

She moaned as sensations hit her. When his tongue probed at her mouth, she opened it, sucked it in, and trembled at the growing arousal.

He growled against her, a soft rumble with only three syllables, "I want you."

She wanted him, too, and this was a dream, which meant she could have him.

Margaret pushed away from him only so she could lay herself down on the plush grass. She opened her arms.

"Take me." Trite and yet his eyes glowed, like literally glowed, green and primal. In that moment, it was if he wasn't just a man but an animal.

Fear made her tremble, but as his body covered hers, she forgot it. Forgot it with the burgeoning passion that begged for relief.

His thigh inserted itself between her legs, and she rubbed against it as his mouth blazed a path from her lips down her neck to her breasts.

As he sucked the taut peak of one, her back arched and she gasped.

"Yes."

He kept suckling at her nipple, and his hand took

the place of his thigh, rubbing between her legs, stroking the wet folds of her sex. Thrusting into her. And she cried out, clawed at the ground, tearing at the grass, her hips riding to meet his fingers. His mouth ravaging her taut buds.

Her climax roared close and—

Beep. Beep. Beep.

The alarm rudely jolted her awake, and disorientation hit her hard. Along with frustration, as her body throbbed. Aching. Needing.

As she caught her breath, she thought of reaching under the covers and finishing herself. Then wondered, did the cameras extend to the private quarters? Lowry claimed they didn't; however, this place held secrets. Secrets they obviously wanted kept. How far would they go to keep an eye on their staff?

She glanced at the ceiling made of suspended pristine white squares with the perforated holes. So many holes, any of which could hide a lens.

Nuts. The company wasn't spying on its employees. The privacy laws they'd be breaking would cost them a fortune in lawsuits.

Or had she signed something indemnifying them?

She'd skimmed through the contracts. For all she knew, somewhere in the mumbo-jumbo legalese she'd agreed to them cataloguing her ever move, her every bowel movement.

Ugh.

Now she didn't even want to use the bathroom, except she didn't have a choice.

The one good thing about wondering if someone watched her pee was it cured her lingering arousal. She managed to keep it under control and thought she'd done a great job until she walked into Luke's room and he said, "Hello, Florence."

CHAPTER SIX

A SHITTY SLEEP LEFT LUKE CRANKIER THAN usual. It didn't help he was hungry. But he refused to eat. Eating would keep him strong. A perfect subject for their tests.

He wasn't about to make it easy for them. He'd already mastered getting his body to ignore the IV nutrients. He could ignore the hunger pangs hitting him as well.

Now if he could only control his dick. He'd woken with a hard-on and not a hand to stroke it.

Down, boy. He couldn't afford to have Sphinx or his cronies noticing his sudden interest in sex. Or was this their fault?

Had they injected him with some kind of erectile stimulator? Given he'd not had issues before now, it seemed plausible.

Well, they wouldn't get away with it. Bad enough

he was a guinea pig for treatment, he wasn't about to stud for them as well.

He willed his cock to wilt. Glared at it until the sheet lay flat once more. A situation that didn't last five seconds when she entered the room, and for some reason, he said, "Hello, Florence."

She recoiled. "What did you call me?"

"Florence, as in Nightingale. If you don't like it, then blame the stupid hat."

For some reason she frowned. "My name is Nurse Henley."

"I don't give a fuck who you are. What are you doing here?" he snapped, pleasure at her appearance drawing irritation, too.

"I work here."

"I told you to leave."

"You did," she agreed, moving to the sink and washing her hands.

"And?"

"And what?" she asked, looking deliciously fresh in a pressed white blouse, trim slacks, and that damnable cap.

"You need to get out of here. This place is dangerous."

"Only if you wander outside after dark. I hear there are beasts in the woods." She dried her hands on a paper towel.

"Did they warn you of the monsters in suits?" They were the more dangerous ones.

"The doctors aren't your enemy. I understand

you're frustrated, but everyone here wants you to get better."

He uttered a short barking laugh. "Don't tell me you believe that shit." She was behind him, out of his line of sight. He couldn't see her, but he sensed her with an uncanny awareness.

"I believe that you're a sick man in need of treatment, and part of that illness is the lack of recognition that there is a problem."

He chuckled. "I know what the problem is, Flo, and it ain't the fact I'm blind to my situation. There are things happening here you don't understand."

"Then explain it to me." She reappeared with a stethoscope and blood pressure gauge.

"If I do, then you'll be in danger."

"From who?" she asked, wrapping the band around his forearm.

"The people keeping me locked up. They'll kill you if they think you know too much."

"Do you realize how crazy that sounds?" She pumped the band and watched the gauge.

"It's only crazy if I'm lying. Which I'm not."

She pressed the stethoscope against his arm instead of replying.

"Nothing wrong with my heart rate," he said as she pressed her fingers to his wrist and glanced at her watch.

"You're right. It's fine." She tapped the results into the tablet then proceeded to grab a penlight from her pocket.

"Must you?" Luke sighed as she shone it in his eyes.

"Your pupils appear fine. Your eyes are brown?" she said almost in a query.

"Most of the time."

She cast him a sharp look. "They change depending on lighting?"

"More like mood." He grinned. "Want to see what color they are when I'm happy?" A waggled brow pursed her lips.

"Do I need to get another wet washcloth?"

The rejoinder brought a bark of laughter. Unexpected and genuine. "Nice one, Flo."

"How did you sleep?" she asked.

"Great."

"Dreams?" she asked, still taking notes.

"Oh yes. A very nice one." Said in a low timbre. "What about you? How did you sleep, Flo?"

For some reason the question brought a blush to her cheek, which caused a chain reaction in his own body.

"Fine." She slapped the tablet back on its perch. "No dreams at all."

An odd statement to make. "What did Chimera want with you?"

She glanced at him for a moment. "To excuse your behavior and then ask me to become your personal caretaker."

"I don't need a fucking nanny," he growled. Especially one like her, who made him feel. He didn't want to feel.

"Maybe you wouldn't need a full-time nurse if you weren't so grouchy all the time," she sassed, heading for the wall. He heard the hiss of the refrigerator seal being broken then the door being shut.

"You try being tied to a bed twenty-four-seven."

"Try not being a dick and maybe they'll let you go." She returned to his view, holding a container with a spoon.

"You don't know what the fuck you're talking about."

"True." She placed the bowl on the tray beside him. "But I've met you, and you're not exactly Mr. Congeniality."

"Because—"

He couldn't say more because she shoved a spoon full of tepid porridge into his mouth. He sputtered. Choked. Spat some out and scowled.

"No food."

"You have to eat," she insisted.

"I'm on a hunger strike."

"How are you supposed to get better if you don't eat?"

"There is nothing wrong with me." A lie. There was plenty wrong, but nothing that could be fixed.

"Oh, I'd say there's plenty wrong, starting with your attitude. Now open wide." She zoomed the spoon, and he clamped his mouth shut.

Glared.

She shook her head and sighed. "Are you really going to make this hard?"

Yes, because he needed her to leave. Now. He resorted to crudity in the hopes of making her flee. "Hard is what I do best, Flo. Pull back the sheet and you'll see."

Her lips pressed into a tight line. Disapproval, with a hint of color in her cheeks. "That is totally inappropriate."

"It is. So, quit. Run crying to Sphincter or Chimera or whoever the fuck makes your schedule and ask to be reassigned."

"You'd like that, wouldn't you?"

"What I'd like is to die in peace."

"Well, that isn't going to happen, so open up for the airplane." She zoomed it.

He glared some more. "I am not a—" He would have said child, but she jammed the spoon in his mouth. He clamped his teeth on it so she couldn't yank it out.

She pulled. "Be a good boy."

Instead he growled and held on.

"Are you really going to make me do it?"

Do what? he wondered but couldn't say anything if he wanted to hold on to the spoon.

She ripped down the sheet, baring his upper chest, which seemed rather promising until she grabbed hold of his nipple and twisted.

"Ow!" he yelled, and she pulled the spoon loose.

"Aha." She dabbed it back in the container while he gave her the evil eye.

She was sly.

Adorable.

And she was waving that spoon again.

"This is abuse," Luke declared.

"As is most of what comes out of your mouth, so I'd say that makes us even."

"Hardly eve—"

More porridge hit his mouth, and this time he spat it out. Then gave her a triumphant look.

She sighed. "Really? You know I'm not leaving until you eat."

"Then you'd better get comfy, Flo."

But his hot nurse wouldn't give in. "Would you prefer a nutrient drip? Because I can hook one up."

"Go ahead and try. It won't work."

"Dr. Chimera said you weren't doing well on them." She gnawed her lower lip.

"Dr. Chimera says a lot of shit. But that happens to be true."

"Well, I am not leaving until you eat."

"Then I hope you brought a change of clothes and a bed because it won't happen anytime soon."

"Surely we can strike a deal," she offered.

"Get me out of here."

"You know I can't do that."

"Then there's nothing to say."

"I'm not giving up."

And she did her best for the next two hours to feed

him. Tried to cajole him into opening his mouth. But he was wise to her games.

He didn't reply, and it appeared that by not baiting her, she didn't resort to torture. In other words, she didn't tweak his nipple or tease him in any way.

Kind of disappointing.

Even more disheartening when she left with a cheery, "See you in a few hours."

No. She couldn't return. He wasn't sure if he could take another bout with her. He'd end up giving in. Eating. Wanting to live. Which would be cruel.

Knowing someone watched, he snapped, "I want a new nurse."

This time it wasn't Sphinx who replied, but Chimera himself, his voice smooth and modulated. "Already? She's just begun caring for you."

"She's mean." And sexy. Not to mention her scent did something to him.

"She is rather assertive and unorthodox in her methods. But I like it."

"You would." Chimera must take pleasure in torture given how he condoned it.

"Why so miserable? I would think you'd be happy I entrusted you into Margaret's capable hands."

Her name was Margaret? He'd only heard her referred to as Nurse Henley. Margaret. A nice name. Did she shorten it to Margie or Maggie? Not that he gave a shit.

"Look at you, thinking about the lovely Margaret. I can see why. She is quite attractive."

"Hadn't really noticed." A lie so big Chimera couldn't fail to spot it.

"Really, Luke, how you could not? Those fine features. Thick hair. For a woman who just hit thirty, she's aging well."

"Thirty isn't old." Look at him, almost thirty-five and fitter than he was at twenty. And that was with no actual physical activity. Imagine if he got free and truly pushed the limits of his body.

"True. Age can be transcended with a bit of help. Science is a wonderful thing. We can cure and fix almost anything."

"For the right price." Because Chimera didn't share his secrets for the greater good. He sold it to the highest bidders. There were plenty. The rich would do anything to extend their lives. To cheat old age. To make themselves better.

They didn't always grasp what a curse longevity and better health came with. Or they did know and just didn't care.

"This kind of research takes money," Chimera replied. "And you and I both know it's not something that should be given with impunity. Can you imagine if everyone received your gifts?"

"Society would implode." In a bloodshed of epic proportions because, for all those who could handle the change in their bodies, their psyches, the essence that made them human, there were those who gave in to the primal beat that thrummed so strongly inside them.

More than a few times he'd given in to his beast,

that monster that lived inside him. The elation proved to be addictive, as was the power and sense of invincibility. But it came at a cost to his humanity.

"I am working on solutions that curtail some of the treatment's more volatile aspects. We're very close to a cure for leukemia."

"Which you'll sell to a drug company for a tidy amount."

"We are no worse than others."

"Does that really help you sleep at night?" was Luke's sarcastic retort.

"I sleep like a man who is next to God."

The worst part? Chimera truly believed it.

"You say you're like other companies." Luke barked a laugh. "Do other companies keep people chained in their basement?"

"We let you walk above ground once upon a time. You could do so again."

"If I behave and swallow the company bullshit. Fuck you." He closed his eyes, as if pretending to sleep would send Chimera away. The man wouldn't be in a hurry to go. He probably sat in a comfortable chair in his office, watching on one of his many screens. He watched everything. No one so much as farted without him knowing how long and how smelly.

Chimera wasn't done taunting. "A shame you're so stubborn. A free man would be able to pursue the lovely Margaret."

"Not interested."

"Your noticeable erections were due to what, then?"

"Urge to pee."

"You were voided during the night when we knocked you out." A reminder that burned. To be so helpless someone shoved a catheter in him and drained him. Then again that was preferable to wearing a bag and having Flo change him.

"Then maybe it was the breeze from the vents blowing the right way," Luke suggested.

"Good to hear you're not interested after all. Then you'll have no issue with me offering her to another."

Anger burned quick and hit within. "She's not a whore to be passed around."

"No, but she does have excellent birthing hips. Did you know that a uterus is still the one thing we cannot recreate?"

The nonchalance of the statement sent a chill. "You are one sick fuck."

"Not sick anymore. I've never felt better as a matter of fact."

Give the bastard one thing, he didn't do to others what he wasn't willing to do on himself. Chimera was his own first patient. What kind of psycho experimented on himself?

One with nothing to lose. Wasn't that why Luke had said yes?

"Blah. Blah. Are you done patting yourself on the back? Because I really don't care. Not about you, your precious treatments, or that nurse," Luke snarled, doing his best to not rise to Chimera's bait.

"You care. Which is why your request to remove Nurse Henley is so amusing. She stays."

"I won't eat for her."

"That is your choice. But each day you refuse, we will slip fertility drugs into her food and drink. When she reaches an optimum point..." Chimera didn't finish his sentence.

He didn't have to.

"I will tell her about your sick fucking operation."

"Then she'll die."

The remark, a chilling one, put an end to the conversation, leaving Luke with a choice when she returned.

Continue on his path to die and make her a victim.

Eat but ignore her charms.

Or the third option, the strange one that appealed to the more primal side of him?

Take the woman and run.

Far. Far. Away.

CHAPTER SEVEN

Dᴜʀɪɴɢ ʜᴇʀ ʙʀᴇᴀᴋ, Mᴀʀɢᴀʀᴇᴛ ʜᴇᴀᴅᴇᴅ ʙᴀᴄᴋ ᴛᴏ her room, noticing Becky's door was only partially closed.

She gave it a light knock.

No reply.

Perhaps she was in the shower. Margaret entered her own room and dropped the plate with the fruit and cold cuts she'd grabbed for lunch on the desk. She wasn't in the mood to deal with the overcast and rainy day outside. Nor was she in the mood to deal with people. Especially the guards who, with the absence of Becky, were chatting her up more than usual.

She'd had enough with pushy men today. Luke had pushed her to the limits of her patience that morning. Acting like a spoiled child. Complaining about his treatment.

Can I really blame him? The man is tied to a bed.

For his safety and that of others.

He didn't seem that dangerous.

Until he smiled. Even a sarcastic smirk had the power to steal her breath.

She wondered if she'd gone too far again with him. Dr. Chimera seemed to approve of her firm approach. Still there was firm, and then there was taking advantage.

Abusing his nipple wasn't in any nursing procedural manual. Anywhere else she'd be fired.

In her defense, she didn't do it hard, despite his surprised yell, and it was for the greater good.

The man had to eat.

Apparently, he'd been refusing. Given what she knew about his diet, she'd studied him more closely this time. Seen a gauntness to his features, an unnatural leanness to his physique.

He appeared to be starving. How long since he'd eaten?

Why did he refuse? A hunger strike, he stated. A form of blackmail to force removal of the restraints. It obviously wasn't working and made her wonder why they didn't keep him hooked to a nutrient and hydration line. He might not thrive with them, but they'd keep his body fed.

Perhaps by forcing him to eat by mouth, they hoped to stimulate his will to live. Because he did have a rather pessimistic outlook.

How long had he been a patient?

She wished she could access the entire file. Dr. Chimera said he'd been injured in a war, which made him a soldier. A man scarred not only by bullets but possibly his experience. Knowing his history might help her understand the man in the present.

I don't need to understand him to do my job.

She wasn't here to make friends with him or to help his mental state. That wasn't her specialty. Caring for him, that was the only thing she had to do.

It would help, though, if every time she looked at him, she didn't remember the dream. If she didn't flush with heat—and desire.

The immorality of lusting after him didn't stop it. Even now, the reminder had her squirming, pressing her thighs tight together. She distracted herself by finishing her lunch, gathering her laundry, and setting her room to right.

Finally, she could delay no longer. Her next shift was about to begin. Exiting her room, she noted Becky's door shut and might have passed by but for the thumping sound.

She knocked. The motion inside ceased.

"Becky?" She lightly tapped again. Worried, given how out of character this all seemed.

"Go away," were the muffled words.

"Are you okay?"

"Fine. Just healing."

"Healing from what?" was Margaret's startled reply.

The door inched open, just a bit. Enough for her to see Becky's left eye. "I had a problem with a patient. It's all cool now."

"What kind of problem?" She shoved at the door, and while Becky initially resisted, she stepped out of the way and Margaret walked in. Gasped.

"Your poor face." Face, neck, and who knew how many bruises under her clothes. "What happened?"

"One of the coma patients woke up. He was a little erratic."

"A little?" was her incredulous reply. "He beat the hell out of you."

"Not his fault. He had no idea who I was. I'll be okay."

"I'm so sorry." Margaret truly was. Had it been Luke? She almost feared asking. He was the only patient she knew in tethers for not being safe. Was this the incident that precipitated it?

"Don't be sorry. This is a good thing. Dr. Chimera gave me a promotion. Said I was wasting my time on the wards. I start in his secret lab tomorrow as his personal assistant."

The acrid jealousy might burn, but Margaret held it in. She wouldn't dwell on the unfairness of Becky getting such a promotion while she got stuck with the hot, angry guy. "That sounds amazing."

"It is." A faint smile.

The watch on her wrist vibrated with a five-minute warning. "Shoot I have to run. My shift is about to start."

"Have fun." Becky waved, and Margaret, anew, had to restrain herself from wincing at the mottled colors marring her friend's complexion.

She walked quickly to the elevator, a bit miffed at Becky's good luck, then feeling guilty. The poor girl had gotten beaten, and only a jealous cow would envy her good fortune as a result.

Rather than jump in the next open cab, Margaret paused and grabbed a few things from the buffet line, packing them quickly in a bag before heading to her shift with only a minute to spare.

The guard had changed since the morning. The man with dark skin and a bright smile— "Just call me Travis, ma'am" with a sexy drawl—didn't take long to check her in. She entered room 602 to find Luke feigning sleep.

She felt certain of it, hence why she ignored him as she bustled around.

Kept banging and moving stuff behind him, where he couldn't see. Purposely making noise. Humming. Heating the food she'd filched from the cafeteria until the aroma filled the room. She'd seen how bland the meal they'd provided for breakfast was. How did they expect to tempt him?

She'd brought a bowl of soup— thick and savory— along with a banana.

She had plans for that banana if he refused to cooperate. Evil plans that weren't part of any rulebook, but then again, nothing about this clinic or situation was normal.

Since he'd yet to twitch or say a word, she moved to stand right behind his head, silently staring at him.

Waiting.

Waiting...

He opened his eyes and met her gaze. Sighed.

"You're a pain in my ass, Flo."

"Not yet, but I'm sure I could manage to find a thermometer."

His lips twitched. "You're not supposed to threaten me with rectal probes."

"You're not supposed to pretend I'm not here."

"Thought I'd spare you a repeat of this morning."

"And here I thought we were having fun," she said as she clicked the button to bring him to a seated position.

"Do you always hurt the people you play with?"

"Only the cute ones."

He blinked in surprise.

Margaret moved, forcing him to find her. He unerringly tracked her with his gaze.

"Buttering me up won't make me eat," he stated.

"Then don't eat. I, on the other hand, didn't finish my lunch, so if you don't mind..." She grabbed the banana and chose to perch herself on the edge of his bed. She made sure her butt wiggled against his legs.

"Can't find a chair?"

"I guess I could use the stool, but this is comfier." She peeled the banana, revealing the pale-yellow fruit. Then she ate it.

She didn't do anything obscene with the banana. Just parted her lips, tore off a chunk, and chewed with happy noises.

He watched her. His gaze fixated on her lips.

Halfway through, she offered it to him. "Want some?" Rather than wait or a reply, she pressed it against his lips.

For a moment, he held firm, and then he parted them. Bit a good inch off. Chewed. She brought it back to her mouth for a small nibble.

His lips parted. She fed him again.

And again, back and forth, their eyes trained on each other, and while nothing untoward happened, she understood she'd crossed some ethical line.

Worst part? She didn't care. Something about Luke demanded more of her.

When the banana was finished, she tossed the peel and returned with the chunky loaded potato soup.

It smelled divine, the bacon and cheese flavoring the air. His nose twitched, but it was his rumbling stomach that betrayed him. She grinned as she sat down, balancing the bowl on her lap. She dipped the spoon and blew on it. Touched it to her lip to test the temperature. Blew on it again.

He opened his mouth.

She ate the first bite.

His eyes widened in surprise then crinkled in amusement. "You don't play fair."

"I didn't realize fairness was involved in sharing my lunch. If you're hungry, I can heat the nutritious meal in the fridge."

A grimace pulled his features. "That's just cruel."

She laughed. "You're right. It is. Here." She filled another spoonful, blew on it, touched it with her upper lip to test the temperature before feeding it to him. He sucked it off the spoon.

The next bite, he shook his head. "Your turn."

She quickly spilled it into her mouth and licked the spoon. His breath might have hitched.

Back and forth they made quick work of it, and before she knew it, the bowl was in the sink and she was washing her hands under cold water and wishing she could have a shower. A cold one.

Because, dammit, she'd only meant to cajole him into eating, not turn the event into some kind of foreplay.

Or was she imagining it, the heat simmering between them? She could easily check. A peek over her shoulder and she'd spot the bulge, if it was there, in the sheet.

Instead, she kept her gaze trained on him the entire time.

With his lunch done, she then found him a drink, the electrolyte beverage in the fridge sipped to the very bottom by her suddenly behaving patient.

She turned to taking his vitals and couldn't help asking questions. "How long have you been a patient of Chimaeram?"

"What year is it?"

"Don't you know?"

He shrugged. "Time moves oddly when you don't have anything to measure it by."

"Twenty twenty-five."

"Wow. Shit." His brow knit. "I've been here longer

than I thought."

"Which is?"

"Not something you should know. How long have you been here?"

"About a month."

"I don't suppose your contract is up soon?"

"Not for another five months. With an option to renew if it works out."

"You should break the contract."

Pausing to listen to his heart, she glanced at him. "Why would I break it?"

"Because."

"Because is not an answer."

"I can't tell you why," he said, blowing out a frustrated breath.

"But on the basis of your word, I'm supposed to just obey." She laughed as she put away the stethoscope. "Yeah, you'll have to do better than that."

"This isn't about obeying; it's about keeping you safe."

"From who? You? Would you really hurt me?" She held his gaze.

"No." Spoken through gritted teeth. "But they will."

"Who is this *they*?" She lifted the bottom of the blanket and ran her finger over the sole of his bare foot, watching his toes curl.

"Chimera, Sphinx, all of them. They see you as a tool they can use."

"Of course, they're using me." She rolled her eyes.

"They hired me. As a nurse." She pointed to her cap.

"You're in danger. And I lied before. You should worry about me. I'm dangerous, Flo."

"There are guards all around. I hardly think I need to worry."

He growled, the sound low and frustrated. Also, more rumbly and primal than she was used to hearing. "You're not listening."

"I am listening to your paranoid delusions. I'm just not taking them seriously. The clinic is here to heal you. Not hurt you or me. Or anyone else. Why just yesterday one of the coma patients woke up.

"Anyone die?"

She blinked at his sarcasm. "No." The one syllable emerged slowly.

"But?" he prodded.

"Poor Becky, another nurse, got hurt pretty bad."

"Another monster for the menagerie. Great." Said in a dull monotone.

"You're not a monster."

"That's because you haven't seen all of me yet, Flo."

"I've seen you naked," she said, and for a minute flashed back to that moment in the dream. Flushed, and suddenly aroused, she glanced at her wristwatch. "Look at the time. Gotta go. See you in a bit."

She moved quickly for the door, but still managed to hear him say, "I saw you naked, too."

The words haunted her until the start of her next shift.

CHAPTER EIGHT

It didn't take long after she left for Chimera to speak. "Well, well, would you look at that. He finally deigns to eat."

"I like potato soup."

"I would have said you enjoyed more the nurse serving it up. I must say I had an urge to have her feed me herself."

Luke recognized the sudden anger as jealousy-based. What he didn't understand was, why? The woman should have meant nothing. He cared about no one, not even himself, and yet he'd given in to Chimera's threat.

"The deal was I eat, you leave her alone."

"Was it? I don't recall. And we really are in need of some healthy wombs. Did you know there's a market for genetically perfected children?"

A low growl rumbled from his chest, and Luke strained at the straps. "Damn you, you promised."

"I did." Chimera's voice lowered. "And I always keep my promises. You should know that by now."

Luke did know.

After he'd signed the contract it didn't take long for Chimera to have Luke moved to his brand-new lab in the mountains. The view was pretty, but Luke hadn't come for the scenery.

Hope brought him. Actually, a helicopter did, but hope got his ass on that chopper.

The room assigned to Luke was small, only big enough for a bit of equipment and a bed. But if what the doctor promised came to pass, he wouldn't be stuck in it for long.

"Why put your clinic in such a remote location?" he'd asked as Chimera bustled around, taking his vitals.

"How could I not? Look outside. See the beauty. Feel the tranquility."

"Notice how no outsiders can get close enough to shove their nose in your business," Luke taunted.

Chimera's lips quirked. "It is much harder for the health inspector to shut us down."

"Is what you're doing legal?" Not that Luke cared. A desperate man didn't give a shit about laws.

"If you're asking if the government knows we're here, then yes. I've been given permission to conduct my studies."

"Studies?" Luke snorted. "Is that a nice way of saying testing on human subjects?" And before Chimera could retort, he laughed. "Listen, I don't mind,

so you don't have to make excuses. I know how red tape halts a lot of shit in its tracks."

"Which is a shame. If you knew all the potential cures currently buried by paperwork and rules—"

"Rules to prevent scientists from playing God," Luke interrupted.

"Those rules are letting people die. Letting people suffer needlessly." Chimera indicated Luke's numb leg. "Do you deserve to suffer?"

For a moment the faces of those he killed flashed in front of him. They screamed yes, yes, he should suffer for an eternity, but he whispered, "No."

"I can fix you. Of that there is no doubt. However, according to the government and their rules, because I haven't jumped through a hundred hoops, you should wait. Then even if we manage to get past the trials, do you know how many cures never make it to shelves because of pharmaceutical companies that bribe the government? They're not interested in cures. There's no money in curing people."

"Are you trying to say you're not interested in money?" Luke made a noise. "I call bullshit."

Chimera laughed. "Oh, I'm in it for the money. Mostly so I can expand my research."

"Speaking of expanding, this place is kind of small." A two-story building with boxes lining the halls and more tarped outside. "Not to mention hard-to-get supplies." Only a small road through the mountains that could disappear with a single landslide. "Doesn't seem like the ideal place to make your mark in the world of medicine."

"What you say is true. This place isn't quite yet ready for all the things I've got planned. But that will change." Chimera stood by the window and stared out. "The work on expanding the labs and facility have already begun."

"Is that why I hear banging and machinery?" As if from a distance.

"We're almost done."

"I don't think I understand," Luke said. "Are you hiding another building?"

"You might say so. The true clinic is actually underground, and it will be the most wondrous thing the world will have ever seen. We will find a cure for everything."

"Seems optimistic."

"It's already happening." Chimera pivoted and pointed to an image on the wall. A man in a wheelchair shrunken in on himself and slumped. "Look closely."

His crutch under one arm, Luke hop-walked over to the wall for a squint. Then a frown as he stared. "Who is that in the wheelchair? Is it supposed to be someone I know?" Because he sure as hell didn't recognize the hunched figure.

"It's me."

"You?" He remembered Chimera saying something about treating himself, but he'd assumed a minor injury. "It doesn't look like you."

"Not anymore. That was when I suffered from motor neuron disease. The same thing that afflicted the genius Hawking. A horrible illness. The body won't cooperate, but the mind...the mind is willing. But trapped. When you've got nothing to plan all day but escape, you find a solution."

"You cured motor neuron?" Impressive feat.

"More like transformed it." Chimera gestured to himself. "I exchanged the effects of the disease for something else."

"For what?"

"That would be giving away my secret." Chimera winked.

"Can you do the same for me?" Luke could have smacked himself for the naked hope in his query. Doubtful they could do the same, given his wounds left deep scars. This wasn't a case of removing a disease. He had permanent damage.

"I guess we'll soon find out. Are you ready to start the treatment?"

Luke was more than ready. He lay on that bed voluntarily. Didn't complain much about the first round of drugs. They made him tired and ill.

Summer passed into fall. The treatments continued, and he felt worse. His body trembled. His moods were erratic.

His thoughts...more bloodthirsty than when he'd served in the war. His impatience grew, as did the pain in his body.

There came a day when he couldn't even rise from

the bed. Sweat oozed from every pore. He was burning up.

As was his habit every morning, Chimera came to see him, adjusting the bag on a pole, a bag with a muddy-looking concoction.

"What's wrong with me? I feel like shit," Luke said through dry and cracked lips.

"An unfortunate side effect. Your body is fighting the change. It will end soon."

It didn't. It got worse. More painful. A man who'd always been brave, he screamed for death. Begged for mercy. Sobbed like the most craven of cowards.

He weaved in and out of consciousness, hating himself. Hope had put him in this bed to be tortured. It was becoming obvious he wasn't going to get better.

The treatment failed. Once he realized that, the next time Chimera came to see him, Luke pled with him. "Kill me. It's not working. Let me die."

"It will work," Chimera insisted. "Your body is just being stubborn."

"It hurts." Luke sobbed, ashamed and unable to stop. "It hurts so much."

"I'm sorry, my friend. Let me help you." The doctor injected something in the IV hydrating his body. "Sleep."

When Luke closed his eyes, winter gripped the land, the swirl of white snow bright in his window. The next time he woke, the leaves were falling from the trees. Which made no sense. Surely, he'd not slept through two entire seasons.

But he didn't hurt.

He was thirsty as fuck, though. He waved a hand around, searching for the table by his bed, not finding a cup or pitcher of water.

A nurse entered, her jaunty cap with its red cross askew, her mouth agape. "You're awake. Doctor Chimera! He's awake."

She sounded shocked. Surprised. Whereas he felt weak. Drained.

Looking down at himself, the frail body under the sheet didn't register at first until he moved his trembling hand to grip the sheet.

His frail hand.

"What the fuck?" He tried to swing his legs out of the bed. They flopped over the side and left him panting with exertion. Before he could test his balance by standing, Chimera was there.

"Slow down, Luke. Your body isn't ready for you to move too fast."

"My body feels like it was run over by a truck, dumped in a river weighed down by rocks." Lethargy pulled at him despite him just waking. "What's wrong with me?"

"We put you in a coma to handle the pain of your treatment. You've been asleep a long time."

"Apparently. How long was I out?"

Chimera's lips pressed in to a line. "Longer than expected. Your body proved resistant to the treatment."

"So I did miss spring and summer."

"You did. It's been almost nineteen months since we induced you."

"Nineteen..." The word whispered from his lips.

"Like I said, longer than expected. Each time we tried to rouse you, the change still gripped you. But there is good news in all this."

"Good how?" He'd lost almost two years of his life.

"Move your leg."

"My leg?" He stared down dumbly at the pasty skin, noting he wore nothing under the sheet. His leg partially hung out. He kicked it. "What about it?"

"Notice anything different?"

It took his sluggish mind a moment before he clued in. "You fixed it."

He began pumping both his legs and then, despite the warning, pushed himself off the bed, stumbling as his knees buckled.

Chimera caught him. Held him upright. "Steady, Luke. Give yourself a moment."

He didn't need a moment to realize the steady pain in his hip from his injury was gone. Actually, apart from the fatigue pulling him and the weakness of his limbs, he felt good.

Damned good.

"I'm healed." He said it softly as if proclaiming it too loud would take it away.

"Mostly. We're not quite done yet with you."

Not done? Did Chimera not grasp what this meant? Luke wasn't infirm anymore. He could do anything, even rejoin the army.

That shining moment still haunted him years later. He should have fled then and there. Or as soon as rehab had him walking and running. But he'd trusted Chimera. Trusted the man's word.

He said he'd make me even better.

Problem was Chimera's version of improved didn't jibe with Luke's perception at all. In the beginning, Luke enjoyed his renewed health, ignored the strange quirks he developed.

But he couldn't ignore what happened to the others. Couldn't ignore the fact that those who tried to leave, to go past those mountains, always returned.

Usually in body bags.

CHAPTER NINE

BECKY'S DOOR WAS CLOSED, SO MARGARET CHOSE to brave the outdoors on her own. The weather hadn't improved. The first wet gust in the face proved it the moment she stepped outside. She didn't let it deter her, moving away from the building, letting the crisp freshness of the air outside fill her lungs. Clear out the stale, recycled air from inside.

It didn't clear her mind.

What did Luke mean when he said he'd also seen her naked? Was he just parroting her words? Because anything else was crazy.

A dream remained just a dream. He didn't share it with her. That kind of thing didn't happen. And even if it did, it wouldn't be with a stranger.

Although he wasn't such a stranger anymore. Her afternoon session with him went better than expected despite her less-than-orthodox methods.

Flirting with him did the trick, even if she cringed at how morally bankrupt that made her. Leading on a patient. The lowest of lows. Yet, it worked. He ate. He drank.

She'd won, and all she had to do was eat a banana and blow a spoon. Not his cock. Really, she hadn't done anything horrible or that sexual even. Now explain that to her body. It protested that she'd brought herself outside in the chilly damp rather than to her room for a quick fix.

A second urge to masturbate and the day only half done. What was happening with her? She'd not been this horny since her teens. What could be the cause?

Luke. His name whispered in her mind.

She shook her head. No. She refused to believe he alone was the cause. More like she'd finally gotten past her intense dislike of men. Funny how a few bad experiences could make a girl totally shut down. It had been months now since her breakup—with that jerk whose face she couldn't even remember—longer since she'd had sex. Not that sex was the be all and end all that people made it out to be. She'd never understood the big deal. She had better orgasms when she masturbated. Still, there was something to be said about having another body next to yours. That intimate contact.

That was why she felt lusty around Luke. It missed that intimacy. The touch of another person, a need she could easily fix. Time to say yes to one of the many offers of no-strings satisfaction.

If only any of the guys around appealed.

None did. Just one man made her panties wet.

The one man she couldn't have. Which probably explained why she lusted. She knew he was off-limits, which made him a safe object to desire.

Despite her actions thus far, Margaret had a line she wouldn't cross. She might indulge in teasing and verbal exchanges; however, she would never go any further. Not only because to do anything would be wrong but also because she was much too aware of the cameras. Hence why she'd kept her back to it while sitting on his bed. Let them hear but not see what she did.

Her steps took her to the soggy field with its muddy running track. She'd not bothered to put on her running shoes, not wanting to ruin them in the mud. She wore insulated rubber boots, the kind that kept her feet warm and dry.

She wore a sweater with a hood she could pull up if the weather abruptly turned nasty. Not exactly the nicest day for a stroll outside; however, given the claustrophobic feeling of being underground most of the day, she felt a need for some exercise. A mindless walk proved the perfect thing, and she followed the beaten track, looping around it, her steps bringing her close to the gray shore of the lake.

The rippling waves, wrought by the smallest of breeze, drew her attention. She approached the lake's edge and stared at it. The edge fell away sharply, the stony bank more of a cliff than a beach. She couldn't see anything today, not with the overcast skies and choppiness of the water. On a sunny day, a person could admire the multi-hued rocky bottom and the fish that swam in its depths. One of the guards swore he'd seen a mermaid in there once.

But no one took him seriously. Mermaids didn't exist.

Just like men invading her dreams proved an impossibility.

With the wind biting through her jacket, she resumed walking, following the mucky trail, her skin and hair dewing with the heavy moisture in the air. It would rain again. The dark clouds promised a downpour, and soon. However, she wasn't ready to entrench herself indoors quite yet.

At the top end of the track, she again paused. Stared at the dense line of forest, less than fifty yards away. She'd never been inside the woods. Rumors of bears were enough to keep her away. She'd heard other stories, too. Tales of creatures that no one could identify. Screams at night. Howling, too.

Possibly tall tales told by men who enjoyed hearing the squeals of women, like Becky, who listened raptly and hung on to their every word.

Monsters didn't exist. But a wolf pack might find her tasty.

As Margaret continued to watch, her skin prickled, the kind of tingle that usually meant someone spied on her. Probably the sniper on the roof. She'd yet to see them actually shoot anything. Which was a good thing. She liked her meat on a plate, well cooked and not hunted in front of her.

The feeble light lessened as the heavy rain clouds smothered the land. She'd better hurry if she didn't want to get soaked. She turned from the woods and began to walk the mucky track. She had only gone a few strides when a sound startled her. A woman's cry.

Did I imagine it? Probably a bird or some other creature.

It occurred again, and she could swear it sound like a plea for aid. She glanced at the forest and gasped. A pale figure appeared to be standing between two thick trunks.

Probably a trick of light and shadows.

Except she could swear she heard a whisper. "Help."

"Is anyone there?" Her feet left the beaten track, and she took long strides toward the trees. The white shape flitted to the side. Not a trick then. There was something there.

Halfway to the woods, Margaret paused. "Hello. Are you okay?"

No reply.

"Do you need help?"

She saw nothing and was deciding whether to move forward or not when the skies opened up.

"Dammit." The rain quickly soaked through her jacket and sweater, making her choice for her. She whirled and began trudging toward the building. Running on uneven and slick terrain would just end up with her splatting ignobly or twisting her ankle.

"Hey." The distant shout brought her chin up, and her gaze sought the building in the distance. She saw the man on the roof, standing, waving his gun.

She waved back.

"Duck," he yelled as he aimed his gun at Margaret.

What on earth? Was he going to shoot?

A noise from behind had her whirling.

Her eyes widened.

What the hell is that?

Something came running at her from the woods, a loping creature on four legs with long, white hair streaming over a humped back. A mouth opened on terrifying yellow teeth. Yet it was the eyes, alight and hungry, that frightened her most.

Those eyes were almost human if one forgot about the fact they glowed amber. But the rest of it...

Monster.

"Oh my God." Whirling, Margaret forgot about any possible injury and began to run.

Crack. Crack.

The gunfire did nothing to stem her panting breath or slow her steps. Did the sniper aim true and take care of the thing from the woods?

She cast a glance over her shoulder and shrieked as she saw the thing, jaw open wide, drool rolling down its chin to glisten wetly. It ululated as it closed the gap between them.

Whirling fully, Margaret faced it, knowing she couldn't outrun it. "Go away. Shoo!" she yelled, hoping the noise would scare it.

As if anything with those wild eyes and snapping teeth would frighten so easily.

When it was still a few yards away, it leapt. She managed to get her arms up to block it. The thing slammed into her hard, knocking the breath out of her, stealing her scream.

Margaret hit the ground with the creature on top of her, its rancid breath washing over her face. She did her best to keep the jaws from getting close enough to chew, her hands trembling as she fought to stay alive. The flesh she gripped was soft and covered in a light, downy fur, and this close, the humanity she thought she'd seen in the eyes was lost behind the savagery.

"No. Please, no. Oh God." She mumbled and keened the words as she struggled, not strong enough to hold it off forever.

The thing managed to rake claws over her cheek, drawing a sharp gasp, but it also gave her a chance, as it only had one front leg supporting it. She shoved her knees under and pushed, managing to heave it aside.

She rolled over and shoved to get to her feet, only to scream as it yanked on her ankle. It felt like fingers gripping her. How was that possible?

She kicked and connected with flesh, causing the thing to utter a sharp howl.

Great, she'd pissed it off. She heard distant yelling

and the crack of more bullets. And here she was standing in the way of the target.

She lurched forward and didn't make it two steps before she was tackled. She bucked and tried to crawl, sobbing and crying out as it bit her shoulder. Her coat afforded protection to her flesh, but the tight pinch would leave a bruise.

She was flipped onto her back and got to see the monster in its full glory. Perhaps it was the horror of the moment or her mind playing tricks, but for a second, amidst the long hair flopping over its face, she could swear the thing smiled and said, "Dinner."

Please, no. She didn't want to die a victim of the wildlife. But she was trembling and weak. The thing knew it as it lowered its head, washing her face with its fetid breath, the hot dribble of drool landing on her chin making her whimper.

There was a distant crack then an awful pause. The creature on top of her froze. Blinked. Its mouth opened and shut without a sound. Through the tangle of hair, Margaret stared at the hole in its head and the slow leak of blood.

It collapsed on her, and Margaret unleashed a scream as she shoved the body off. Scrambling to her feet, she ran for the building, ignoring the men in black fatigues jogging past her. She gasped for breath but didn't stop running until she was inside the safety of the four walls. Her knees gave out at that point, and she dropped down, heaving in deep sucking breaths.

"Nurse Henley." The familiar voice drew her from

her stupor, and she stared almost unseeing at the man kneeling before her. "Nurse Henley. Are you okay?"

"No," she blurted out. She was most definitely not okay. "There was a thing." She held back before calling it a monster. Yet what else fit?

She'd never seen the like. Not even on TV. She still had difficulty comprehending it. Like most animals, it ran on all four legs and yet there was something lopsided about its gait. Something strange about it period. Especially why it decided to attack.

"You don't have to worry. The creature is dead," Lowry said, his voice low and soothing.

She shivered at the reminder. She, who'd seen countless gunshot wounds, would probably have nightmares of the one that happened right before her eyes.

"What was it?" she said through chattering teeth.

"Initial reports from the guards in the field indicate some kind of hybrid beast. Reminiscent of the chupacabras down south."

"It didn't look like an ugly dog. It appeared almost human."

"Simian is the term you're looking for," Lowry said, correcting her.

"You're trying to tell me that thing was a monkey?"

"Of a sort. Like I said, it is a hybrid creature, probably a mix of wolf in there, too."

The very illogic of his statement did much to calm her, and she snorted. "Monkeys and wolves do not make babies together."

"Not under normal circumstances, however, as

mentioned, we are in a protected ecosystem where the choices for mating are limited. In such a situation, it is possible," Lowry explained.

Did he really think her that gullible? She knew how biology worked. Yet, he seemed quite serious. "Even if it were possible, how did a monkey get here?"

"Again, not a monkey, but a simian creature. Common to these mountains and that most likely spawned the Sasquatch stories prevalent in these parts."

"Are you saying that was a Bigfoot?" She held in a hysterical giggle.

"A hybrid version, yes."

The laughter, a high-pitched sound, escaped. "Now I know you're screwing with me."

"I assure you, I'm quite serious. They're rare, which is why they mate with other species. Unfortunately, their offspring are erratic creatures."

"I'll say. That thing wanted to eat me. I didn't think Bigfoot was a carnivore."

"Their diet is varied."

"Are they why we're not supposed to go out at night?"

"Yes and no. They are only one example of the dangers roaming these mountains. We are merely visitors in an untamed landscape. It is why we have such strong cautions about straying into the woods."

"I wasn't in the woods. It came after me." The reminder brought the fetid warmth of the breath back to mind.

Lowry kept his gaze calm and steady. "Usually they avoid exposing themselves in the daytime; however, the overcast skies—"

"In other words, my fault for going out when it was almost dark." She sighed. Something dripped on her hand, and she looked at the red drop of blood with a moment of incomprehension. "It scratched me."

"The infirmary should be able to do something to prevent infection and ensure there is no scarring."

"Is it that bad?" She brought her hand to her cheek, and it came away wet. With blood. She also noticed throbbing in her body, especially her shoulder where it bit her.

Lowry helped her to her feet. "You'll be fine. Do you know where to go? Do you want me to accompany you?"

"I'm going to be late for my shift." Not that she felt like dealing with Luke. She just wanted to huddle under a hot blanket with a rum toddy.

Lowry uttered a soft chuckle. "Such a good nurse. But tonight, you are the patient. Forget your evening shift. Get patched up. Rest. You can resume your duties in the morning if"—he held up a finger—"and only if you feel well enough. You had a traumatic experience. It would be understandable if you required a day or two to recover."

"I'll be fine." She was alive, not seriously injured, and the thing was dead. She still felt the weight of it on her when it died.

As she moved past Lowry, the door to the elevator

hallway buzzing her through, she turned around and caught a glimpse of the soldiers returning, a limp body carried between them before the door closed. The head of the hybrid creature dangled down, the hair a white snarled nest, and in that tangle, a pink plastic barrette.

CHAPTER TEN

SIXTY. ANOTHER MINUTE PASSED. A HUNDRED AND
ninety-two since she'd left. Luke had kept count mostly
to ensure he was ready for Flo this time. He'd had time
to give himself a pep talk.

I will stay in control.

No more stray erections.

I will insult her until she leaves.

Because having her stay wasn't an option.

No more eating.

Eating made him strong, made him think about life
beyond this bed.

With all those resolutions made, he found himself
impatiently counting the seconds and minutes and
hours until the door opened.

His attention perked at the click of locks disengaging. Given she'd left him in a seated position, he faced
the door, ready to blast her with something rude.

But it wasn't Flo who entered.

"Chimera." He growled the name.

"Once upon a time, you called me Adrian," reminded the other man, looking as slick as ever in slacks and a dark silk shirt open at the neck.

"You mean back when I thought we were friends."

"Despite what you think, we are friends."

"Friends don't experiment on each other."

"Not true. It's almost a rite of passage in the teen years and college to fool around with new experiences."

"Don't make light of what you did."

"What I did?" Chimera repeated. "You agreed. You gave me carte blanche to do anything to make you whole again."

"I didn't say you could make me your lab rat."

"Need I remind you that the only reason you're in here, locked up like an animal, is because of your actions."

"Still punishing me because I tried to escape."

"You did more than escape," Chimera snapped. "We never did recover most of the subjects and without treatment..."

"They turned into monsters. Which isn't my fault. You're the one playing God with lives."

"Are you going to start this argument again?"

No, because there was no point. What was done couldn't be changed. Chimera saw himself working for the greater good and never mind the people he destroyed along the way.

"Why are you here?" Because Chimera rarely

visited these lower levels. He preferred to watch and manipulate from above.

"I thought I'd inform you in person that Nurse Henley won't be coming this evening due to an unfortunate incident."

Luke tried to surge out of the bed, but the restraints held him back. Not so his snarled words. "You bastard. What did you do to her?"

"Me?" The innocence was real not feigned. "I did nothing to the lovely lady. However, an outdoor excursion did lead to her having an encounter with a predator."

"Is she okay?" His heart stilled at the thought she might be grievously injured.

"Shaken mostly."

"And the thing that attacked her?"

"Dead."

"One of your failures?" he asked with a sneer.

"No one is a failure. Everything we've done has taught us something."

"Did it teach you how to not be an asshole to other human beings?"

"The science we are exploring is bigger than a few lives."

"What happens when that science turns on you?" It could happen. Not all humans handled the treatments the same.

"There is no one size fits all," reminded Chimera. "What we do here will revolutionize the future of medicine."

"And who cares if you kill a few people on your way."

"We don't treat the healthy, you know that. All those we choose are grievously damaged in some way."

"Is that supposed to make it all right?" Luke said with sarcasm. "Because I'm gonna tell you right now, it's not cool."

"Everyone who receives treatment volunteers."

"Only because you don't give them the entire truth."

At that, Chimera's expression hardened. "Are you telling me that had I told you there was the possibility you might lose yourself to madness it would have stopped you?"

The truth was Luke would have done anything for the hope of being whole again. "I'm done talking to you." Because the conversation never changed. "If you're done giving your message, leave."

"Actually, I'm not done. It occurs to me that perhaps Dr. Sphinx was rather harsh in his punishment of you after your last attempt to escape. And it has been weeks since it happened." Chimera flicked a finger at the restraints. "What do you say we take these off?"

"Do it." Luke's lip curled into a smile. "Right now. I dare you."

Chimera laughed. "Not me. And not here. Too much equipment worth too much money. I'll have you moved first. Tonight, while you sleep. Tomorrow, or the day after at the latest, you'll be a free man. To a certain extent, of course. Can't have you roaming quite yet, riling up the staff and other patients."

Luke didn't trust the sudden benevolence. "Why untie me? You know I won't behave. What are you up to?"

"You said it. We were once friends."

"I'll kill you if I get the chance."

"You wouldn't be the first to try." Chimera moved to the door. "Now if you'll excuse me, I'm off to check on Nurse Henley. To extend my deepest regrets at her unfortunate incident."

"Stay away from her."

"Such concern. One would almost think you cared."

"Fuck you."

"Wouldn't you rather fuck the lovely nurse? Maybe you'll get a chance tomorrow."

"Don't you dare send her to me. You hear me, Chimera? I want a new nurse. She's mean." All lies, but did Chimera buy it?

"Me thinks you doth protest too much about the attractive nurse. Whatever shall you do when your hands are free tomorrow?"

Free to touch... He feared what might happen.

"I don't want to be let loose. Keep me tied. I don't want your fucking freedom."

There was no reply as Chimera left, the door locking behind him. Luke growled at the empty room. Tugged at his restraints. Ignored his growling belly, which played traitor now since it had eaten once.

What game did Chimera play? Because no doubt he had some end game in mind.

Before Luke could fully replay their conversation and suss out the missing piece, the hiss of gas began. They were putting him to sleep early tonight.

He fought it. Did his best to stay awake, only to succumb, falling into a dream.

A dream of a vast green field, too perfect and artificial. Muted sunlight. And Flo.

As before, she cocked her head and said, "Why are you naked again?"

He glanced down at himself—his body whole and unmarked, his cock well represented—and grinned. "Why aren't you?" He was rather intrigued by this new element to his drugged sleep.

She wore a nightgown this time. The cottony kind that resembled an oversized t-shirt. The cat graphic on the front being of some scraggly critter stating, "Where's my coffee?"

"Put some clothes on," she demanded, averting her gaze.

"Make me," he said with a smile. "You keep saying this is your dream, which means you're the one turning it into something dirty and erotic."

"I don't have erotic dreams," she primly stated.

"Then you've been missing out."

"This feels so real," she remarked.

It did, and it was funny she mentioned it. "But it's not, which means we can do anything we like, and no one will know." Last time he got a kiss and fingered her. This time, maybe he'd get even luckier.

Her chin lifted. "I'd know, so don't think that argument will get you another kiss."

"So you remember our last kiss."

"A dream kiss," she said. "Which doesn't count."

Perhaps not to her, but it had lingered with him when he woke. "If it doesn't count, then there should be no issue sharing another."

He took a step forward, and she retreated, shaking her finger at him. "Oh no you don't. I am not in the mood. Especially not after what happened to me."

That brought a frown. "So it's true, you were attacked?"

She looked startled. "You know?"

"Chimera told me. Are you okay?"

She hugged herself, her eyes taking on a haunted cast. "No."

An urge to wrap his arms around her, to make promises he couldn't keep, filled him. "He said you weren't hurt."

"I wasn't, not really. Just superficial stuff. But it was scary. Its face..." She shivered.

He moved toward her, and she didn't retreat this time as he said softly, "It's dead now. It can't hurt you."

"But there are others in the mountains. Lowry said so."

"Not all of them are savage."

"Says you. How many Sasquatches have you had to fight off?"

He frowned. "Who called them Sasquatches?"

"Lowry did. Well, actually he said the one that attacked me was some kind of hybrid. A Bigfoot slash wolf mix."

"And you believed that?"

She shrugged. "Not really, but it does make some twisted kind of sense. What else would explain why it appeared somewhat humanoid? Legends have claimed for a long time that Sasquatch are real."

"They're not Sasquatches, nor hybrids," he retorted. "They're what happens in this place when the doctors get the dosage wrong and go too far."

"I don't understand. People, not even doctors, can change a person into something else."

"Not the ethical kind," he muttered.

"What are you saying? That the thing in the woods was human?"

"Forget it." He wasn't here to discuss the annoyances with himself. Because this was just a dream, and no matter how real Flo seemed, she remained but a construct of his mind. As such, it meant he could reach for her and draw her into his arms.

"What are you doing?" She didn't move out of his embrace.

"Holding you."

"Why?"

"Because."

"I thought we discussed 'because' not being an answer." Her lips quirked.

"Would you feel better if I said I wanted another kiss?"

"Do you?" she asked.

More than anything. "Maybe," he hedged.

"I'm your nurse. Kissing, even hugging like this," she said with a cock of her head, "is crossing too many lines."

"They won't punish you. How can they when this is but a dream?"

"But a dream too real. What if I forget when I wake, and I do something stupid when I see you?"

"Stupid how?"

Her lips pressed tight.

"This isn't real, Flo. And I'll prove it. Let's exchange a code word. Mine will be octopus."

She frowned at him. "What's saying octopus supposed to do?"

"Next time we see each other, I'm gonna look you straight in the eye and say octopus. And it won't mean shit to you because this is a dream."

She snickered. "My dream, which means I should have the secret word. And I choose filet mignon."

"A steak?"

"Tastier than an octopus."

"Ever had them breaded and fried?"

"No, and I have no intention of doing so."

"You're missing out."

Since held her loosely in his arms, this proved to be the strangest conversation. On the one hand, his desire for her remained, but he also quite enjoyed the bantering. Even if he did imagine everything, it was a welcome relief from his shitty life.

"Do you ever have family visit?" she asked randomly.

"Nope. None of the patients do. We're specially chosen because of our lack of ties. No close family, or friends." He'd shoved them all away from him after his injury.

"Me either. My parents were old when they had me. As for friends..." She blew a breath. "I accepted a nursing job in Edmonton, met a guy, and well... It didn't end well."

"He hurt you." He clenched a fist and practically growled.

"Yes and no. He hurt my feelings. And I'm over it. Just wish I hadn't been so stupid and seen what he truly was."

"He hid the monster inside," Luke murmured, turning away from her. Just like he was hiding right now. The fact that this was a dream didn't negate the fact he, too, carried ugliness. A beast.

A real one. He never could forget that. This dream made it all too easy to pretend, though.

She touched him, just a light press of her fingers on his arm. "What's wrong?"

"I'm bad for you, Flo. You're right to shove me away."

"I'm doing it because I'm your nurse. It wouldn't be right for us to get involved."

"Even if you weren't my nurse, we couldn't. I'm broken, Flo."

"You don't look broken. I see a man who is whole and healthy."

"You're not seeing everything."

She moved to stand in front of him. "These feelings you have. The negativity. The anger. There are people you can talk to. Medicines you can take."

Laughter snorted from him. "I don't think there's a pill to fix what ails me, Flo. I'm a monster."

"Oh, Luke." She lifted her hand to cup his cheek, and he couldn't help but close his eyes and enjoy the touch. Even if imaginary, it was more kindness than he'd felt in a long time.

"I meant what I said before, Flo. You need to get out of here. Before it's too late."

"Too late how?" she asked. "You worried another one of those hybrid things will come after me? Because you shouldn't. I won't be going anywhere near those woods."

"I don't want them doing to you what they did to me. Don't let them change you, Flo. Don't trust them. Don't trust the food. The water."

"You're letting the paranoia take over, Luke. You need to fight it."

"I'm not paranoid," he snapped. "It's the truth." Which, even in his own dream, no one believed.

"No, this is part of your illness. Part of what Dr. Chimera is trying to fix."

Sharp laughter met her statement. "I'll bet he is. He's one of the reasons I'm so fucked."

"What happened to you?" She slapped herself in the forehead. "What am I doing? Asking you for answers when this is only a dream."

"You want to know my biggest mistake? I should have said no when Chimera offered me the deal, and yet instead, I let myself be tempted. I didn't read the fine print. Hell, I didn't care. I was so desperate for a miracle. What happened to me is my own fault. I am my own worst enemy. But it soon won't matter."

"Why?"

"Because I'm going to die."

"No. Don't say that."

"I have to. It's the only way out."

"Stop it." The slap took him by surprise, especially since the sharp crack of it stung.

"Ow. What the fuck, Flo? I'm really beginning to wonder about your bedside manner."

"And I am tired of your pity party."

She thought he was whining.

Okay, so maybe he was. But he had a right. "I'll fucking bitch if I want to. You've seen my life. My prison."

"Only because you keep fighting. Did it ever occur to you that maybe if you cooperated, that you'd be set free?"

Her words echoed those of Chimera and the others. However, he knew them for a lie. "They'll never let me go. I'm too valuable to them."

"Are you sure of that? Or are you afraid to try because they might free you and you'll have to actually live life on your own?"

He blinked at her. The logic so off-base he couldn't believe his subconscious even spewed it. "I am not afraid to live."

"Then fight. Fight to get better. Show the doctors you can do it. Show me."

"There's only one thing I want to show you, Flo."

Her lips quirked. "I've already seen it."

"Ah, but you've yet to feel it."

Funny how dream Flo could blush like the real thing. "I wish you wouldn't say stuff like that."

"You mean tell you how attractive I find you. How you're the only thing I look forward to right now."

"You're just grateful for—"

"Oh, fucking shut it. I have the hots for you, Flo." He dragged her near, close enough to capture her mouth before she could argue some more. Again, just like the real thing, just like kissing her felt real.

The mesh of their mouths electrifying. The soft yield of her lips groan-worthy.

Once he rid her of the nightshirt, their naked bodies fit so well together. So right.

In his dream, he didn't have to worry about the monster he'd become. He could kiss a beautiful woman, cup her full ass, grind his cock against her belly.

Gasp in disappointment as she pushed away from him.

"I hear my alarm." She cocked her head. "I'm going to wake up, and I'd rather not be horny again."

Again? His lips quirked. "This dream only ends when I wake, Flo. Not you."

The claim didn't stop her from fading from sight, leaving him alone in a verdant green field with a massive erection.

And two free hands.

He fertilized the grass.

Twice.

CHAPTER ELEVEN

WHEN SHE ARRIVED ON LEVEL SIX, HER CARD
didn't work for the ward. Holding in a sigh, Margaret
was about to press a button for help when the door for
Ward C opened and the guard from the day before
emerged.

"Hi. My card isn't working," she said, gesturing to
the locked portal.

"Your card was probably reprogrammed."

"Have I been reassigned?"

"No, but the patient has been moved," the
guard said.

"Moved? Where?" And why had no one had said
anything to her?

"If you'll follow me." The soldier led the way
through the door he'd emerged from, down a long hall.
At the end, another locked door, which the guard
opened, leading them into a large antechamber with
another pair of guards. All armed.

She moved toward the next door, but the guard held up his hand. "A moment, please, ma'am." The door they'd just passed through closed and locked before the man stepped aside.

"You may now proceed."

How gracious of him—not. She found herself curious about the changes. "Since when does Luke require so many guards?"

"It's because of the new room."

"Is there something wrong with it?" Wrong enough it required extra security?

"The chamber itself is secure enough. We're here as a precaution given Dr. Chimera left orders that you could remove his restraints if you feel it's appropriate."

"I get to decide?" It seemed a no-brainer. Free him. Until she reminded herself that the dream Luke she kept kissing wasn't the real one. The real Luke was dangerous. She just had to look at the guards dispatched for one man to realize it.

"If you're ready to enter?" The guard inclined his head.

Ready and not ready, if that made any sense. It didn't. Just like the sense of anticipation confused. Her vivid dreams were bleeding into her reality, making her feel things that weren't real.

She focused on the here and now. "Why does Dr. Chimera want me to release him?"

The guard shrugged. "He doesn't explain his decisions. I am just the messenger."

A messenger that advised her that she held Luke's freedom in her hands. For a moment, she debated turning on her heel and marching to Chimera's office to ask more questions. Such as, why her? Why not Luke's doctors or the guards themselves? Why leave her with the choice to release him or not? She didn't want that power.

Margaret approached the door and frowned as she noted it took two guards, each with a hand on opposite scanners, to unlock it. The third stood behind her, and while she didn't peek, she would wager he had his hand on his gun again.

A glance to either side showed the guards with fingers resting on the grips of their weapons.

Ridiculous precaution, given the fact, when she entered, she noticed Luke strapped to a new bed, one made of concrete that molded into the floor. He was immobile, and yet they were all so scared.

Again, why? She wished someone would tell her what to expect.

Luke didn't say anything as she entered. Did he sleep? More like he faked it again.

"Morning, Luke."

"At least you didn't add the usual 'good' to it." He opened his eyes, and she only met his gaze for a brief second before turning away.

"Are you having a bad day?" she asked, checking out his new room, frowning at the starkness of it.

"No worse than usual. But I hear you had a shit night."

The reminder brought a shiver. "Just a few scratches from a wild animal attack."

"Let me see," he insisted, craning his head, this bed not lifting him to a seated position like the previous one.

"It's nothing." She lifted a hand, self-conscious of the bandage on her cheek.

"Did you need stiches?"

She shook her head. "Doctor Cerberus says it should heal without a scar. He put cream on it."

"Nothing else? No shots? No special drinks?"

She frowned. "No. Should I have had a shot? Do you think it had rabies?"

"You can't catch it. We're not contagious."

"We? You're not a wild animal," she remarked as she washed her hands and checked out his new quarters. Unlike the last room, this one was bare. No machinery. Not a single trolley with tools.

"I'm dangerous, Flo. More animal than man."

"Don't be silly. You might have impulse control issues, but there's nothing bestial about you." The walls appeared seamless except for one handle. A yank on it showed a compartment with a tray of food. A cardboard tray, she might add, no utensils. She pulled it out and placed it on the tall, rectangular concrete table, again molded into the floor, as were the stools.

Nothing he could grab and throw. It still didn't mean she'd decided to untie him.

"Which shows how little you know. Don't untie me."

"Excuse me? Are we trying reverse psychology now?"

"I know Chimera told you to do it. Don't deny it. I see how you keep looking at my cuffs and biting your lip. You're not sure you should. Listen to your gut instinct. Leave me tied."

"Why? I thought you wanted your freedom."

"I do."

"Are you worried you'll hurt me?"

He snorted. "I'd never harm you. But I can't guarantee I won't touch you. It's harder than I thought, separating dream from reality."

The fact he said the thing that mirrored her own issues gave her pause. "Have you been dreaming of me?"

He didn't reply.

"Luke?" She took in a deep breath, calling herself all kinds of crazy but still said, "Filet mignon."

He sucked in a breath. "What did you say?"

"Nothing." She felt stupid for thinking it even possible. She was rummaging around the wicker basket, noticing the towel and cloths when he said it. Barely a whisper.

"Octopus."

She froze. "I hate octopus."

"Only because you've yet to try it breaded and deep fried."

She whirled, her eyes wide with shock. "So it was—"

He shook his head. It didn't take a genius to realize

he didn't want her to say anything. Electronic eyes watched, and someone surely listened. What would they think if she and Luke were to discuss their shared dreams?

It was nuts.

Yet it had happened. There was no other explanation.

The fact there existed a bond between them, even a strange one, was what decided her. She put her hands on the restraint for his left wrist.

He growled. "What are you doing?"

"Letting you go so you can eat. You'll choke if I try to feed you lying down."

"I can do a great many things on my back, Flo. Climb on top and you'll see." He leered in conjunction with his blatant proposal.

But she finally grasped it for what it was. A way to alienate her. She finished undoing the buckle.

He grimaced. "Stop it. I said no."

"You're not my boss." She moved to the other side and removed the other cuff. He lay prone, his arms still in the confines of the leather straps.

"Put those back on."

Instead, she took care of his torso strap then his ankles.

He said nothing. Didn't have to. The tautness of his body said it all.

"This is a bad idea, Flo."

"Yeah, well, it wouldn't be the first one. So do me a favor and don't make me regret this."

He sighed. "This won't end well."

"Only if you're an ass. Are you coming to eat?"

She perched herself on the round seat of the stool, the hard concrete not the most comfortable thing. It took him a moment before he joined her, wearing bottoms she noticed. Someone must have dressed him before moving him to this room.

She gestured to the offerings. "Orange juice." In a box, no straw. "Fruit." Banana, apple, and strawberries. "Bacon." She snatched a piece and chewed, saying in between nibbles, "Blueberry toaster waffles."

"Would it kill someone to give me a goddamned coffee?" he grumbled, but that didn't stop him from poking a hole in the juice and drinking it then pretty much eating everything in sight.

Not that she minded. She'd had a light breakfast before showing up, and it pleased her to see him eating. Hopefully the bosses watching noticed.

"So I'm not sure what I'm supposed to do next. They didn't leave me any instructions or tools," she remarked when they finished. She snared the remnants of their meal from the table and disposed of them in a narrow chute for garbage

"I believe the intent is for me to seduce you and impregnate you with my mutated sperm to see what kind of child we might create."

At his preposterous claim, she blinked. "You have a vivid imagination."

"Not really." A smile hovered on his lips. "I simply know how their minds work."

"If you're so good at reading them, then how come you're stuck down here?"

"Because I didn't feel like playing their game." He shrugged. "Their version of freedom and mine didn't jibe."

"Who's paying for your treatment? Are they the ones insisting you stay here?"

"No one is paying. Not specifically for me at any rate. This is an institute run entirely on donations. There are people with money expecting great things from Chimera and his cronies."

"So is this a research institute or a healing clinic?" Because she'd yet to figure that part out. She asked even as she knew she shouldn't. Chances were someone watched and listened. Still...she'd finally reached a point where she felt a need to know.

"Both. It's an experimental research clinic."

"A secret one. Which means we shouldn't be talking about it."

He snorted. "What else should we discuss? The fucking weather?"

"It's overcast again today."

"I wouldn't know. I haven't seen daylight in a long fucking time."

"Would you like me to ask if we can take a trip to the surface?"

"Contingent on my good behavior?" He offered her a crooked smile. "What if I don't want to behave?"

For some reason she blushed. Glancing away from

him, she busied herself wiping the crumbs from the table.

With breakfast and cleanup done, she didn't know what to do with herself. "I don't see any of my usual tools for taking blood and stuff."

"Because you're not supposed to be my nurse. I told you, they're hoping we'll do the horizontal tango."

"I don't believe you."

"Really? Ask Chimera. Or Sphinx."

"You're being foolish." Said with a shake of her head. "No one is trying to make you breed. You can't let your delusions control you."

"Delusion?" He arched a brow and mouthed, octopus.

The reminder of the shared dream almost swayed her.

Almost.

Then she remembered where she was. With a patient. In a clinic. "Yes, delusion. Adrian isn't—"

"Adrian, is it?" Luke interrupted with a snarl. "I didn't realize the pair of you were so cozy."

If Margaret didn't know better, she would have said he sounded jealous. Then again, it was possible. Nurses often became an object of affection for patients. It was up to her to ensure it didn't go any further. "We are coworkers, and as such, the use of first names is permissible. But we are not involved as you're implying."

"You'd better not be."

"I don't think that's something you have a say in."

"He's bad for you."

"So is a box of donuts. But whether I indulge or not is still my choice."

Luke rolled his eyes. "Oh, for fucks sake, Flo. Don't be an idiot just to spite me. Stay away from Chimera. Stay away from everyone here."

"Everyone, except you?" she replied.

"Even me," he snapped. "I still meant what I said. You should get out of here. Before it's too late."

"Too late for what?"

"I can't say."

"Because your paranoia is part of your illness." Never mind she wasn't sure what he was sick with. Surely his strange ranting was part of it. "No one is out to get you. No one wants you to make mini Luke babies."

"Did it ever occur to you that maybe I'm not bull-shitting? What if I could prove it?"

"The very fact you're willing to talk about it shows me it's fake. Don't you think if the clinic were involved in something nefarious, they would stop you from telling me?" She'd seen enough movies to know what happened when someone talked. The nurse died.

Yet here she was alive and well.

"What do you know?" he asked. "What could you tell?"

She could tell someone of the pink barrette. She shuttered that thought. More than likely the creature had found it and, like a magpie, collected it.

"There's nothing to tell."

"There is; you just haven't connected all the dots. And in a sense, it's probably better you don't. Then you'll lose even the semblance you have of freedom."

"You're rambling."

"I'm trying to make you understand. These doctors, they want something from you. From us. Why else assign you to me? Why else untie me? If Sphinx had his way, I'd be in a permanent coma like those on level four."

"Those comas are trauma induced, not intentional."

"You keep telling yourself that, Flo."

Which made her think of the third IV. What was in those tubes? "I'm not leaving, Luke. I signed on to do a job, and I am going to do it."

"Okay, Flo. You want to make the bosses happy? Take off your clothes."

She snorted. "Not happening. I'm a nurse, not a prostitute."

"A nurse who has no nursely duties to complete. Because you're not here to care for me. You're here because I got a boner when you touched me. And now all the watching doctors want to see me fuck you."

"No, they don't." She shook her head, shocked by the crudeness of his statement, but even more disturbed by her body's reaction.

"Let's test your theory, shall we?" He moved toward her, a stealthy, stalking aspect to his step that had her backing away. She didn't stop until her back hit a wall. Nowhere to go and he kept advancing until he stood before her. Hotter than her dream. The real-ness of him caused her breath to shorten.

"What are you doing?"

"Proving a point."

"By what? Scaring me?"

"Actually, I'm going to kiss you. Kiss you long and hard and I guarantee that no one watching will stop us."

"You can't kiss me."

"You can't stop me."

Nor did she want to. Surely, she wouldn't feel the same electric connection as they shared in the dream.

He neared and bracketed her with his arms.

Any moment, she expected the door to open or a voice to demand he step away.

He leaned down, his face close to hers, his breath brushing her lips.

"Don't you get it, yet, Flo? They're using you to get to me."

"Why?" she whispered back

"Because they finally found a weakness."

She was his weakness?

She might have asked him to explain, except his mouth caught hers in a kiss. A torrid touch of his lips that stole all thought and breath.

It was better than a dream. Better than anything she'd ever imagined. She tasted the lingering sweetness of juice on his tongue. Her senses were drugged by his scent, the musky aroma of a man whose heated body pressed against hers. The hardness of his erection rubbed against her belly, causing a chain reaction. Moisture pooled between her legs, and her sex quivered with need.

Want...

His hands skimmed down her arms, and he reached around to grab her by the ass. Tugging her even more closely into him.

The door slammed open, a disorienting noise that had him growling as he spun her away from him. Standing in front of her, his body bristled.

She could understand why. All three guards confronted him, weapons drawn.

"Your timing sucks," Luke snapped.

"Move away from the woman."

"Don't you lay a hand on her." He advanced on them, clearly worried about her, and yet, it wasn't her in danger.

Pfft. Pfft. She heard the odd pops and saw his body jerk. Luke slumped to his knees.

His head drooped, his slurred words barely discernible. "Guess I was wrong, Flo."

Then he hit the floor.

CHAPTER TWELVE

For a half second, Margaret stood frozen. Disbelieving. They'd shot Luke!

No. Oh no. She dropped to her knees and could have sobbed in relief when she realized he breathed. Flipping him over, she expected to see blood, and lots of it, only she blinked.

Luke hadn't been shot. Not with bullets anyhow. Darts stuck out of his chest, so many of them. Surely too many for one man.

"Why did you do that?" she cried, yanking at the capsules, throwing them to the side, hoping to prevent some of the drug from overloading his system.

"Just obeying orders, ma'am. We're going to need you to exit the room so we can secure him."

"Like hell am I leaving. Don't you dare touch him." She partially covered him with her own body. "You had no right to shoot him. I had things under control." A total lie. She'd lost complete control, which meant this was her fault. She should have pushed Luke away rather than get caught up in the moment.

"Ma'am, you need to vacate the room," the guard said, a note of impatience in his tone.

"I am not leaving my patient." She stated her intention firmly. They didn't give her a choice. The guard reached for her, the iron grip of his fingers biting into her arms. He managed to haul her away despite her struggles and curses.

"I am going to talk to your boss about this," she screeched as they released her in the hall.

"Go ahead," smirked the tall one. "He's the one who told us to tranq your boyfriend."

Adrian gave the order? The gravity of what had happened hit her. She'd let a patient kiss her and been caught doing it. She'd be fired for sure.

Yet she didn't let her own culpability douse her anger. Without waiting for an invitation, she stormed to the upper levels and banged on the wall where Chimera's office door hid. For a moment, she thought it would remain shut against her. She banged it again, and it abruptly slid open, almost dumping her on the floor.

Regaining her balance, she held herself tall and addressed the secretary. "I need to speak to Dr. Chimera."

"You don't have an appointment." Said with tight lips and a disapproving tone.

Margaret didn't let it deter her. "I don't care. You tell him I want to speak with him right now." Because she needed to explain herself. Needed to apologize so they wouldn't fire her and take Luke away.

"You can't just barge in and—"

The inner office door opened, and Adrian stood within the gap. "It's okay, Janine. I'll see Nurse Henley." He extended a hand. "Please, come in."

She swept in full of righteous anger and ignored the seat.

"Why did your soldiers attack my patient?" She didn't bother with niceties.

"They hardly attacked him. The sedation won't harm Luke and will wear off in a few hours."

"It wasn't necessary," she snapped.

"The man assaulted you." Proving Adrian had been watching. The very idea made her skin crawl and once again roused the question of, how far did he take his spying?

"I'm unharmed. Luke only kissed me." Only. Understatement. That single moment had branded her and now had her confronting the man who, with one word, could have her escorted from the premises. No job. No money. No Luke. However, she couldn't back down now.

"A forced embrace is considered assault. We don't allow our patients to take liberties with our staff. We acted to protect you."

Which she should be grateful for. Any other patient who tried a kiss, she would have welcomed the help—and he'd have probably earned a slap. Problem was Luke wasn't just anyone. And a part of her realized that her anger stemmed from the fact she didn't want the kiss to end.

"I would have handled it."

"And if you couldn't?" Adrian said with an arch of his brow. "We had to act quickly lest something more unfortunate occur."

Her lips pressed into a line. So much for Luke's theory that Adrian and the other doctors wanted him to impregnate her. "Does this mean you're going to put him back in restraints?"

Chimera shrugged and spread his hands wide. "What else can we do? Barely out of them an hour and he acted very inappropriately."

"He merely tested boundaries."

"And you were allowing it. Did I make a mistake, Nurse Henley, in assigning you to Luke?"

The questioning of her professionalism stung, especially since it was valid. "I thought you liked my unorthodox methods. I've got him eating, in case you hadn't noticed."

"I noticed, which is the only reason we're even talking. I am, however, concerned that you're developing an emotional attachment to the patient."

"You speak as if it's wrong to care."

"Caring is fine. It's when it crosses a line that it's not. We are a medical institute that prides itself on providing the finest care for its patients. I won't have a foolish crush jeopardize my work."

Crush? The verbal rebuke slapped, and the last of her anger drowned in her shame.

"It won't happen again, Dr. Chimera."

"Please ensure it doesn't, Nurse Henley. You're excused from duty for the rest of the day."

"What about Luke?"

"He'll be taken care of."

Words with an ominous ring. She left his office, head ducked rather than meet the disapproving glare of his secretary.

What had she been thinking? Luke kissed her, crossing all kinds of boundaries, and she crossed even more by not stopping it right away. Adrian was right. The soldiers did need to interfere since she lacked the common sense to do it herself. But they didn't need to shoot so quickly. They could have talked to him first. Asked him nicely to move away.

Or was she being foolish?

Adrian seemed to think Luke posed a danger. Had they not stopped him, would he have gotten violent?

He wouldn't.

Or so Margaret would like to think, but then again, what did she really know about him? The fact they might share dreams didn't make him a good man, and she really had no assurance he wouldn't hurt her.

Nothing but her gut, which said he wouldn't. Given her gut's previous track record when it came to men, she should thank her boss for putting a stop to the kiss.

Entering the habitat level for employees, she noticed a lack of commotion, the televisions silent for once, no one hanging around.

Entering the women's wing, she noticed Becky's door open, the tunes playing loudly. She poked her head in and peeked around. Didn't see her friend and walked in farther.

"Becky?" She wondered if the woman was feeling any better since the attack.

The bathroom door suddenly opened and released a waft of steam. Becky stepped out, wearing a towel and slick wet hair. She also screamed. "Jeezus, Margie, what are you doing barging in?"

"Your door was open, and I wanted to check on you."

"Aren't you just a doll. I'm fine. Whatever the doctor gave me worked ah-may-zing," Becky sang, swinging her face left and right, the skin showing only the faintest hint of yellow.

"Wow. That's awesome." Bruising as deep as Becky had should have taken days to heal. Maybe even weeks.

"Isn't it, though? They are doing some amazing things here, Margie."

Lifting her hand to her bandaged cheek, Margaret had to wonder what she'd see when she peeled off the bandage. "I'm glad you're feeling better."

"Never better. And just an FYI, I'm not going to be around as much."

"How come?"

"I'm going to be working more closely with Dr. Chimera on a secret project. Since he sometimes works late, some nights I'll be staying in his personal lab. He's got a room set up with a bed and everything."

"That seems odd."

Becky's face twisted. "Nothing odd about it. You're just jealous he's chosen me to be his confidant and assistant."

"I'm happy for you, really I am. Just make sure you get some down time. Wouldn't want you to be overworked."

Becky tossed her auburn hair. "It's not all work. Most of the time, it's just sitting around, keeping an eye on his rats."

"Is he experimenting on them?"

The other woman pressed her lips into a line. "You're trying to get me to spill secrets so I'll get fired."

"What?" The accusation startled. "No. Just making conversation."

A strange expression crossed Becky's features. A suspicion that appeared out of place given how good-natured she'd had always been. "I think you should go."

"Okay. Good luck with the new assignment," Margaret said as she exited the room. Rather than reply, Becky slammed the door behind her.

The conversation left her unsettled. What was Becky doing for Adrian? She really wanted to know and not because she was jealous. She might not always like the girl, but she wouldn't want to see her abused.

Especially since Becky might not be mentally stable. What happened to the girl she'd met on the helicopter? The happy, bubbly woman who laughed at life and was full of curiosity and eager to share it? Had she stopped taking some meds?

Or was it a side effect from the remedy that took away the bruising?

Suddenly feeling a little queasy, Margaret entered her room and headed for the bathroom. She stared for a moment at the bandage on her cheek, the stark whiteness of it taunting.

Pull it.

Her fingers gripped the edge, and she hesitated. Would it be gone like Becky's? Would she, too, begin to act strangely? Indulging in paranoia. Luke also had that problem. Was that a flaw in the remedy?

She tore free the bandage and was almost relived to see the red line on her cheek, not as angry as expected, but definitely not miraculously healed.

Her body slumped as she gripped the edges of the sink. What was wrong with her? For a moment, she'd almost given in to paranoia, too.

"They're not doing anything weird," she said aloud. Everything was just fine. Luke was a damaged man, and as for Becky, she must have some kind of bipolar condition. Maybe she'd forgotten to take some pills, or she was feeling the effects of isolation. Hell, maybe it was that time of the month making her bitchy.

Rather than reapply a bandage, Margaret chose to leave it exposed. Entering her room, she paced. Too restless to sit. The walls of the underground facility felt close, too close, and yet her heart raced at the thought of going above ground.

The face of the monster flashed in front of her, and she couldn't do it. Couldn't go to the surface.

Which left her where to go? The common room where she might have to socialize? Not interested.

She'd been told to take the day off, and yet she'd prefer to work. She heard a door slam. Becky leaving for her shift. For some reason she opened her door and peeked out. She saw the ass end of her friend moving quickly up the hall.

Curious, Margaret followed. Was Becky off to work in the super-secret lab? Was it on the same level as all the others? What exactly was the clinic working on? Luke kept hinting at bad stuff, but Becky seemed to think otherwise.

Becky didn't pause when she reached the junction for the wings. She turned left.

Not right to the elevators, or even straight ahead into the men's quarters.

Why was she going toward the unfinished section?

Just before the corner, Margaret flattened herself against the doorway. Before she could peek, she heard a whirring sound. How strange. She waited, counting to thirty and then glanced around the corner, looking into the third opening, the empty opening.

No Becky.

Impossible. Becky couldn't have vanished in thin air, and she'd not come back this way, which meant she must have entered a room.

What room? There was no door for the unfinished corridor, simply rough rock blocking it.

More curious than ever she traced Becky's steps down the hall under construction, noting the lack of doors and hiding places. The rock wall brought a furrow to her brow.

Becky had disappeared.

Impossible. Which meant there must be a logical explanation.

She placed her hand on the rough surface and felt a slight hum. Sliding her fingers over the rock, she gasped when her hand disappeared from sight.

She blinked, especially since it made no sense. She saw her arm, most of it, but the wrist and hand appeared buried in rock. She waved her other hand through the hologram, disrupting it enough to see a black panel, the kind that required a card to activate.

A hidden entrance.

One that Becky had access to. No preventing the jealousy from consuming her this time. While she was getting reprimanded for unprofessional conduct, Becky —with her mood swings—was the head doctor's assistant. Which made her wonder what Adrian did in his secret lab that required a nurse.

Boredom and restlessness dogged her the rest of that day. By the time she went to bed, she welcomed the dream—and Luke.

"Are you okay?" she asked, noticing him immediately but somewhat disappointed he appeared for the first time wearing clothes.

"It's not the first time I've been put to sleep." He scrubbed a hand through his dirty-blond hair. "What time is it?"

She shrugged. "I don't know exactly. But if it helps, I went to bed at nine."

"PM?" he exclaimed. Then grumbled. "Of course, it's nighttime, and I've yet to wake, which means he's upped the dosage of my meds. Fucker."

"I'm sorry about what they did. It's my fault. I should have never let you kiss me." She took the blame.

He mocked it. "Don't you dare apologize, Flo. Kissing you was worth it. What's surprising is the fact Chimera stopped it."

"I told you there was no plan. I saw him after. He actually got mad at me. I thought I was going to get fired."

"Don't you dare start apologizing." Having ducked her head, she didn't see him approach but felt his fingers grip her chin and lift it. His gaze met hers. "I wanted to kiss you. Just like you wanted to kiss me."

"That doesn't make it okay. I'm your nurse."

"No, you're not, because I'm not a patient. I'm a prisoner."

"I'm sure it feels that way." It also looked it, too. But saying so aloud would only feed his delusion. Why did crazy have to be so sexy?

"For fuck's sake, Flo. When are you going to start admitting to yourself that this place isn't what it seems? They're doing experiments here. On humans. Doing shit you can't imagine."

"You mean like healing impossible injuries?" She arched a brow. Having seen what they did for Becky, she was starting to believe, and yet, they'd not used the same remedy on her. Why?

"They might be healing, but in doing so, they're changing us in ways that nature never meant."

"How? What have they done to you that's so horrible, Luke? From what you told me you could barely walk before. The pain was intense. Now, you're whole, healthy. What do you have to complain about?"

"I'm not a man anymore."

"There are pills for erectile dysfunction."

That caused him to blink before blurting, "Fuck me, I'm not limp dicked. Which you should know by now."

She did. "So what do you mean then when you say you're not a man?"

"I'm a beast."

"I'll admit you can be crude, but you're hardly an animal. I thought we already discussed this."

He rubbed his face. "And you still don't grasp the truth. There's a monster inside me, Flo. A dangerous one, like the thing you met in the woods."

"That thing in the woods was an aberration."

"So am I." He said the words low. Serious.

It hurt her inside. She reached up to cup his cheek. "You're not a monster." Then before he could say anything more, she leaned up on tiptoe and kissed him.

CHAPTER THIRTEEN

Luke froze for a moment as she initiated the kiss. Her lips soft against his. Their touch tantalizing. Which made him wonder how he could feel in a dream. He didn't understand why this happened. How had this crazy connection between them formed?

What was it about Flo that drew him? That brought them together as if they belonged with one another?

Fate.

The word whispered at him, the rightness of it, of her, the only real thing in his life at the moment.

A life that was no life.

He broke the embrace and spun away rather than gaze upon her and give in to the temptation.

The light touch of her fingers on his back made him tremble.

"Don't," he said, his voice tight and low.

"I thought this was what you wanted."

He sighed. "What I want I can't have. We can't be together, Flo. It's dangerous."

"Not in here it's not. No one will know what we do."

She thought he feared discovery? He shook his head. "I don't want to hurt you."

"Why would you hurt me?" She moved around to stand in front of him, once again confronting him, her hair loose in soft waves around her shoulders. For once she didn't wear that stupid cap. She did, however, wear clothes. Damnable things.

"Being with me could have an adverse effect. I don't think I'm contagious, but there's much about what they did that's still new."

"What did they do? You keep talking about it. Like they changed you. Changed who you are. But no one can do that." She pressed her hand to his chest. "Inside. Here. That's you. Only you."

"That's just it, though. They did find a way to pervert what I am. Their treatments pulled something primitive into the light. Some days it's a struggle to not let it take over."

"But you're fighting it. And winning. Let me help you." She cupped his face. "I want to help you."

He couldn't push her away. Couldn't say no the sweetness of her embrace. Couldn't resist wrapping his arms around her and holding her tight to him.

He lay her down on the grass that filled the field of his dreams.

Their clothing melted without need for fumbling. Their naked skin pressed together.

Luke let his lips brush hers, a soft rub of sensual exploration. As if the explosive passion between them could ever be so tame. She wrapped her arms around his neck and held him close.

Part of him knew he should push her away. This had gone too far. She refused to listen when he tried to warn her; however, he couldn't resist the pleasure.

Couldn't resist the touch of her. The feel of skin on skin. The acceptance.

Their lips meshed, devouring and nipping eagerly. The slip of her tongue into his mouth wrought a groan.

Beneath him, her body undulated, moving against him, her hips pressing upwards, seeking the friction he could provide. But he kept his cock tucked between them. He had to remind himself to go slow, lest he lose control.

This might be a dream world, and yet, it felt real. Real enough he had to be careful.

Luke let his lips trail from hers, and she made a noise of disappointment. Only to sigh in pleasure as he licked his way down the smooth column of her neck to her collarbone.

So fragile. The pulse of her racing heart a flutter below the skin. He pressed his lips on it and closed his eyes against the urge to bite.

Bite.

Mark.

The need proved hard to resist. Yet he was a man, not a beast to bite a woman.

He kissed her and moved on as her fingers tangled in his hair. He moved lower, drawn by the vision of her perfect nipple. The rounded breasts jutted proudly for him, the taut peaks begging for a taste.

He drew a nipple into his mouth, sucked it, and Margaret moaned loudly as she arched her back, asking him for more. He sucked. Swirled his tongue around the tip. Delighted in the way her buds peaked. Luke turned his attention to the other one, biting it gently, lavishing it with the same sensual tease. A slow seduction at odds with the grinding need in his loins. He wanted to slide between her soft nether lips, fill her with his cock, and fuck her until she screamed his name and raked nails down his back.

But what he wanted even more was to bring her pleasure. To prove he could remain in control, even as her every sigh and moan sought to destroy it.

As he continued to kiss and suckle at her breasts, Luke reached down, letting his fingers stroke their way up her thigh until he reached her soft curls.

The sound she made drew his eye, and he stared, transfixed by the beauty of her. The perfect image of a woman aroused with her eyes closed in rapture, her lips parted, and her skin flushed.

He dragged his fingers through her curls and cupped her mound. Her hips rolled, thrust against his hand, and she whispered, "Taste me."

With pleasure. He moved himself that he might lie

between her legs, his head at the apex of her thighs. His view incredible. Her pink lips glistened with honey. He kept watching as he used a finger to touch her, sliding a finger in.

Tight. Hot. Wet.

Eager. Her hips arched against his hand and pumped at his finger. She wanted more.

He could give her more.

He dipped his head and lapped at her while he finger fucked her. Toyed with that button of hers, sucking at it until it swelled, and she sobbed his name. Sliding a second finger into her as he pulled at her clit with his lips. Hearing her cry out as her sex clutched his fingers tight, her orgasm rippling hard enough to almost make him come.

And when the waves in her channel ebbed, he inched his way up her body, kissing her along the way until he found her mouth. He reveled in her soft pleasure cries, swallowed them even as his hand worked to rouse her again.

She undulated against him, her breathing ragged, her skin flushed.

"Now," she begged.

Which was enough for him. He didn't have to fumble with a condom, not in a dream. And they were both naked.

Ready.

He braced himself over her, bracketing her with his arms. He caught her gaze, their eyes locked, and he wondered what she saw. Did his eyes glow with passion? Did she feel how tenuous his hold was on his primal side?

But he couldn't stop. Not with her eyes half-lidded with passion, her lips parted on soft gasps, her hands clutching at his hips, urging him on.

As their lips meshed, the head of his cock nudged the entrance of her sex, and the heat of her brought a groan. He tried to go slow, determined to enjoy every moment, every slick slide of flesh.

But she was tight. So tight.

Hot. Oh, so hot.

And she was impatient. She bit his lower lip, causing him to rear, driving his hips forward, meeting her own thrusting up. The thick length of him sheathed inside her body, stretching her, fisting him.

He might have let out a sound that was more beast than man as he gave in to pleasure.

There were no words, no more soft staring, just unbridled passion. His hips thrusting, pushing, driving deep, hard, fast.

And she met him stroke for stroke, her fingers digging into his hips, her body undulating against his.

At the peak of their passion, he opened his eyes and saw her watching him.

Her lips parted, and she whispered, "Your eyes. They're glowing."

Here was to hoping his cum didn't because he came with a howl, his head rearing back, his hips grinding forward.

And she cried out as her own climax hit, and it was

his name she yelled.

His. Name.

As his seed spilled into her.

His dream seed and yet he felt a deep satisfaction. A sense of rightness and belonging.

She's mine.

There was no more room for doubt. No more room for arguing.

What they'd done had cemented it. But he said nothing to her as he collapsed to the side and drew her near. He held her in his arms and watched over her as she fell asleep in the dream. But he remained awake.

Watching.

Thinking.

What now?

Things had just changed. A bond was forged between them. Forget sending her away. He needed her with him. Which meant...

He awoke, suddenly, the bright lights in his room blinking on and Sphinx bellowing, "Rise and shine, buttercup." Ignoring the man, Luke lay on his concrete bed, made barely tolerable with the foam mattress.

No more did he want to shut down and die.

Nor did he want to do anything that would keep him away from Flo.

Time to play the game. To abide by the rules.

Because only then would their vigilance slack. And he needed that to happen. The time had come to plan an escape.

And he was taking Flo with him.

CHAPTER FOURTEEN

Waking with a smile, Margaret started her day with a shower—her hands running over sensitized skin. What a dream last night.

Luke proved to be a firm, yet gentle lover. Taking care of her pleasure before his own. Holding her tenderly in his arms after. Was it any wonder she smiled?

Problem was doubt kept trying to steal her happiness.

Luke remained a patient. One convinced the doctors were out to get him.

What if he's telling the truth?

Even if he were, what could she do? She was a nurse with no way to contact the outside world. If she did, what would she say? For all that the clinic was remote, there was no possible way Chimera operated without the government knowing.

Which, in turn, meant someone sanctioned his actions. Whatever those actions were.

Truly, how bad could they be given they'd healed Luke? Perhaps in time Luke would accept it instead of casting doubt on the methods.

Thinking of Luke brought a happy tremor to her body. She looked forward to seeing him, despite knowing she couldn't do or say anything to indicate it. She'd almost been fired for her actions. She couldn't afford a single misstep.

I need to be a pro. To pretend as if nothing ever happened and hope they kept meeting in their dreams.

And making love.

Was it wrong to wish the day would pass quickly into night?

Leaving her room, she stopped in the cafeteria long enough to pack a large breakfast, enough for four people, before she headed down to level six. The closer her steps brought her, the more she had the urge to grin. Her excitement proved hard to contain. Who knew dream sex could be so satisfying? The best part? No one knew or could accuse of her anything because she'd never actually touched him.

However, she did wonder if he, too, had the same dream. The fact that they knew each other's code word might have been some weird fluke. Perhaps last night was a one-sided thing.

Entering his room, she bit her lip, especially since the guards covered her back, hands on their weapons.

She found Luke sitting on a stool, dressed in loose

scrubs, not tied up as she feared. His expression was serious. No hint of the lover until he winked. "I don't suppose you brought me some deep-fried octopus?"

"Scrambled eggs and bacon are your treat for today."

"Any honey?" The query spoken with a naughty curve of his lips.

It brought a blush and allayed any fear she had that the dream was one-sided. It made her more eager for the night.

They played patient and nurse that day. Both behaving as they should. Holding back from stray touches, overlong looks, and any kind of talk that might be construed as something more.

It was torture. Especially since she couldn't immediately fall asleep that night. But when she did, he was there. His arms open wide. His touch electrifying.

They did this for days. A week.

Two.

Slowly but surely, she got to know him, not just the places he liked to be touched in their erotic dreams, but the Luke before this happened. The child neglected by his parents. The man who fought for his country.

And in turn, he learned of her. Of her older parents, who died and left her alone in the world. Of her asshole ex, a man Luke growled he'd like to kill—a vow spoken so vehemently she shivered because she believed he would.

It proved a perfect time, and a strange one as well.

In public, AKA his room in front of the camera, they were perfectly behaved.

But at night, when she closed her eyes…she became his wanton lover. With a sex life more satisfying than she could have ever imagined.

Problem was this interlude of happiness, this impossible thing between them, couldn't last forever. It preyed on her sometimes in between her shifts, the time she spent alone. It didn't help she had no one to talk to. Becky was rarely around with her new duties, and most of the other staff were standoffish. Except for the men, but they wanted only one thing.

The dreams took a toll on her, almost as if her waking time in them counted. She sure as heck felt tired. More and more each day. She blamed the fatigue on her health issues.

For the last week she'd felt bloated, slightly nauseous as well. Her breasts were tender. All symptoms of her period coming and yet she'd just finished it. She wasn't pregnant. Dream sex had that going for it at least. However, she couldn't deny feeling run down. Perhaps she needed to spend more time outside. She'd only gone briefly since the incident, and when she did venture forth, she stuck close to the building and kept a wary eye on the woods.

She'd heard of no other incidents. It seemed her encounter was a random, if unlucky, occurrence, and yet, she couldn't shake the nagging fear.

At the end of the third week, she arrived for her

afternoon shift to find twice as many soldiers as usual standing outside Luke's door.

"Is something wrong?" she asked, recognizing most of them. Derek, who always looked so damned serious. Peter, with his short-cropped blond curls. Martin, with his ebony skin and always-present smile. The fourth soldier was Jett, only seen a few times, his dark looks matching his demeanor. The man had no sense of humor. Then there were two others rounding out the group, their faces familiar, probably seen in the communal area of the habitat level.

"Nothing wrong, ma'am. We've got orders to escort you and the patient topside."

She blinked. "You're letting him leave the room? Under whose orders?"

"Dr. Chimera said his good behavior has earned him an hour outdoors. Under guard, of course."

Of course. As if they'd trust him to behave. Did they suspect the sham she and Luke perpetrated each day? Whatever the case, Luke was going to be allowed more freedom. She couldn't wait to tell him.

When the door opened, she found him reading a book of all things, stretched out on his bed, one arm tucked under his head. He appeared much more relaxed these days, the simmering anger he'd first exhibited mostly gone, although he did keep his sense of sarcasm. As to his digs about the clinic and the doctors running it? Those he saved for their time together in dream world. Which meant those watching truly believed him a changed man.

She couldn't deny a certain pride and pleasure in thinking that she was the reason for that difference.

Hearing her, he put the book aside and sat up, offering her welcoming smile. "Right on time with lunch. I'm starving."

It had become part of their routine that she brought him more palatable fare from the cafeteria. She waggled the cooler bag packed with their meal. "Right here, but we can't eat it right yet."

He groaned. "Why not? I'm wasting away, Flo." The clasp of his stomach and groan brought a giggle.

"It will be worth the torture, I promise. We're going to have a picnic."

He smirked. "Because sitting on the concrete floor is so much more ambient than the concrete stools."

"I meant a picnic outside."

The shock didn't show in his expression, but his body stiffened. "Outside?"

"Yes, outside, as in under the sun and sitting on grass. Dr. Chimera gave permission for you to enjoy some fresh air for an hour. That is, if you want to?"

"Does a bear shit in the woods?"

Her nose wrinkled. "I assume that's a yes."

"Yes, it's a yes."

"It will be under guard."

He waved a hand as he swung his legs over the edge of the bed. "Yeah, yeah. Whatever. Please tell me it's sunny."

"Very." She glanced at his feet. His bare feet. She knocked on the door and stood back, waiting for it to open. Derek appeared in the doorway, the other guards ranged behind him. "Ready, ma'am?"

"Not quite. We need shoes for Luke."

"I'm fine, Flo."

"No, you're not fine. You need shoes." Which took a little maneuvering, especially given his rather large feet, but one of the new guys eventually returned with a pair of plain sneakers that fit.

During it all, the door remained open, Luke sat on his bed patiently, and none of the soldiers were trigger-happy. How things had changed for the better. Hopefully today's excursion would be the first of many, which, in turn, would help his healing. He still persisted in his insistence something sinister was going on at the clinic. While she didn't necessarily understand the unconventional methods, she couldn't deny the results. Level five was at full capacity with patients woken from their comas. As was level six. Not that she had anything to do with the other nurses or patients. Luke remained her sole charge.

But it just went to show that the clinic was doing good, no matter what Luke thought. And today, he'd finally see the doctors only wanted him to get better.

Shoes on his feet, thick sweater for him and her, eventually she deemed him ready and off they went, two guards leading the way, another on each side, and two behind. She tried to pretend they weren't boxed in and hoped Luke didn't notice the guards had their hands on their holsters.

During their trek, Luke remained placid. Behaved.

Anyone spying would assume him the perfect patient, but she knew him now from the shared dreams. Knew that he longed for nothing more than to escape.

She had to wonder if he'd try this first excursion outside. And if he did, would she let him?

Would she let him flee without her?

During their dreamtime together, he'd mentioned his plan as they lay entwined in each other's arms.

"I'm going to escape one day."

"To go where?"

"Anywhere the doors have no locks and there's a window I can look out of." He then rolled her atop him, so their gazes aligned. *"I want you to come with me."*

"Run away with you?" The very fact he asked filled her with warmth. Then reality poured cold water on it. *"But my job. My life."* If she ran, she couldn't return to it.

"You'll get a new job."

"I guess I could. A nurse can work anywhere."

"Do you need to prove you're certified?"

"Of course, otherwise anyone could claim they were capable."

He shook his head. *"Sorry, Flo. But if we run, you'll have to change your name. We can't have them tracking us down."*

"But nursing is all I know." It was also something she'd worked hard for. *"Why do you have to run? Surely the doctors see how well you're doing. I'm sure they'll release you soon."*

"I told you, Flo, they'll never let me go."

He truly believed it, and at times, she did, too. Because, despite those patients who'd woken, she'd yet to hear of any leaving.

Could be she just wasn't privy to their departure given she didn't care for them.

Or maybe he's right and they never leave. Maybe there is something weird afoot.

Luke's paranoia proved contagious.

As they exited the elevator to the main level, the tension in the guards ratcheted up a level. Their bodies betrayed their tenseness as they moved through the doors to the antechamber.

Luke couldn't hide his excitement. When the door opened, he squinted at the bright, streaming sunlight. Then stepped out into it, hands extended, face upturned, basking in the rays.

The sadness hit her suddenly as she understood, in that moment, he truly was a prisoner. No matter the intentions of the doctor, there was no reason to hold him here. No possible excuse for not letting this man be outside.

As they stepped away from the door, he breathed deep. "I'd forgotten what real air smelled like."

She had to swallow the knot of tears. "I hope you don't mind the feel of real grass since I didn't bring a blanket," she remarked as they walked away from the concrete ringing the building to the grassy area by the lake.

"I love the feel of grass on bare skin."

There was nothing overtly sexual about the words,

and yet, she knew what he said. He reminded her of their dreamtime. When he would lie on his back and she rode him.

"Keep your clothes on," grumbled Jett.

"Don't worry, dude, I won't show you how inadequate you are," smirked Luke.

Margaret rolled her eyes. Men. Always comparing penis size. Inwardly she smiled at the fact he jested. Much better than fighting or trading truly vicious barbs.

The soldiers spread out into a wide circle as she found them a spot by the water, the scrubby grass ending at the large rocky edge. She sat down, plopping the packed lunch beside her.

"Lake is gorgeous," he said, standing and staring at it.

"Cold too, so no swimming."

"It's not the cold you need to worry about," he muttered. "Did you know this lake is several hundred feet deep?"

"Aren't they all?" she replied as she unpacked the food.

"The sides to this lake are almost sheer instead of sloping like most. Most likely an underground cavern collapsed, hence the sharp drop-off."

"Here's to hoping nothing more collapses given the clinic is built not far from it, using more of the underground cave system."

"Convenient given it keeps it from prying eyes."

She wondered at his brazen words, until she realized none of the soldiers reacted.

"Relax, Flo. They can't hear us. Which means I can say things like I wish I could peel those clothes off you and kiss every inch of your body."

"Luke!"

"I'd let you keep the hat on."

She shook her head at his temerity, her cheeks heating. Another glance at the soldiers showed all but one looking outward. Jett, however, stared at Luke. Who, being a shit disturber, blew him a kiss.

"Don't antagonize them," she hissed.

"Just having some fun, Flo. Chill."

"I'd rather this day not end in your butt getting darted."

"You and me both, but I think we're good." In between bites of food, he spoke in a low murmur. "Chimera's up to something."

"Have you spoken to him?"

He shook his head. "There has to be a reason he's letting me outside."

"Recognition of your good behavior?"

He snorted before taking a bite of his thick sandwich. He kept an eye on the soldiers nearby, close enough to act, but far enough to not hear his murmurs. "He wants me to escape."

"How do you figure that? Six armed guards. I'd say it's the opposite."

"I can handle six."

"But you're not going to. You just got your outdoor

privilege. Which I take as a good sign. Maybe he's getting close to letting you go."

"Don't be gullible, Flo. He's playing us."

"Or you're being paranoid again."

Luke sighed. "I wish you'd believe me, Flo."

"I believe that you believe what you think."

"In other words, you think I'm nuts."

She chose her words carefully. "No, I think you're a man who doesn't easily trust."

"I trust you."

"Then listen to me when I say patience. Today you're outside for an hour. Maybe next week, you'll be able to move around without a posse."

"The minute those guards take their eyes off me, I'm gone."

"Gone where?" She didn't gesture to the mountains, knowing they were watched, but she did say, "There are no roads out of here and you can't exactly hijack a helicopter."

"I don't need a road. I've got two legs and a keen sense of survival."

"Please, don't do anything rash. Not yet. Give it a little more time."

He glanced away from her. "I can't promise you that, Flo."

He didn't say much after that, lying on his back, sunbathing in the late fall sun. She knew he was a little angry at her for not encouraging him. But really, how could he expect her to condone such a crazy idea?

These mountains were considered impassable for a

reason. Not to mention, there were wild animals in them. There was no point getting into a heated argument about it now. Not with guards watching. She'd try and work on him tonight when they dreamed. Perhaps use her feminine wiles to sway him. The very thought caused another blush.

She leaned over, lying on the smooth rock edging the lake. It felt nice to be outdoors again and, even better, not panicked. It helped she not only had Luke beside her but six armed guards. Nothing could get her. She was safe.

The clarity of the water beckoned. She trailed her fingers in the water, causing a ripple effect that made it seem like a shadow moved under the surface.

A shadow that grew...closer?

She leaned down to look, her fingers still in the cold water.

Was that a curious fish? The strange shape neared the surface.

Before she could remove her hand, something grabbed hold of it and wrenched her in!

CHAPTER FIFTEEN

FLO UTTERED ONLY A TINY SQUEAK BEFORE SHE was yanked under.

And he meant yanked!

Jumping to his feet, Luke scanned the water while the guards shouted.

"What the fuck took her?"

"Get him inside," barked another.

"Save her, motherfuckers," Luke yelled. Why did none of them dive in?

Because they were afraid. Loaded down with heavy clothing and gear, the water arctic in temperature, and whatever took Flo to contend with.

Luke didn't have such constraints or fear. It took only a second to kick off the shoes and dive in.

The water proved brisk, shockingly so, and his core temperature plummeted.

But he didn't care. Through the clear water, he

could see Flo struggling, pulling against the tentacle wrapped around her arm.

He kicked toward her, even as bullets peppered the water.

Fuckers were shooting at him.

Luckily the liquid slowed the bullets enough they passed harmlessly by. He kept swimming, kicking hard.

When he reached Flo, he wrapped his arms around her and added his strength to her struggle. To no avail. The appendage remained tightly wrapped around her arm and her mouth, agape, her eyes wide with fright. Not a bubble emerged.

She was out of air. She went limp, and Luke knew he had to do something. Releasing her, he grabbed the tentacle, the flesh of it rubbery. Before he could think twice about it, he opened wide and bit down hard.

The spongy texture reminded Luke of his dislike of raw seafood; however, he had no other choice. Flo needed him. Flo would die if he didn't save her.

He kept chomping, ignoring the squirt of fluid, holding on tight despite the wild thrashing. When the tentacle finally loosened its grip, he quickly grabbed Flo and headed for the surface, his own lungs ready to burst, his body cold. Oh, so cold. And Flo. So still. Lifeless.

Too late.

No!

He emerged from the water and sucked in a deep lungful of air. The guards shouted, and hands reached for him as he kicked towards the rock. He let them yank Flo from the water, even let them drag him forth.

He shook them off as soon as he hit firm ground. Ignored their shouted orders. Let them shoot him. He couldn't stand by and do nothing as Flo lay there, her skin a waxy blue, her chest not moving.

He grabbed hold of her and turned her on her side, whacking her on the back, emptying her mouth of water.

Flipping her back, he began mouth-to-mouth, still ignoring the commotion and orders to stop.

Fuck that.

He used his own breath to expand her lungs. Used his will to silently chant, *Breathe. Open your eyes. Do something. Live. Dammit all, Flo. You can't die on me now*.

Despite the threats, the guards didn't shoot, nor did anyone stop him from blowing into her mouth over and over as he applied chest compressions.

Only when she twitched, then coughed, did he rock back on his heels, his hands deftly rolling her that she might wretch out the lake water. So much fucking water and coughing and more liquid.

"Jeezus, Flo. Did you have to drink the whole lake?" His shitty attempt at humor.

He heard someone shout, "She's breathing."

Fuck yeah, she was breathing, because she wasn't allowed to die. He scooped her into his arms as she weakly said, through teeth that chattered, "What happened?"

She'd almost died. Because of something in the lake. Something that shouldn't exist.

"You went for a swim," was his reply. Not that she heard. Her eyes fluttered shut, and her head lolled to the side as deep shivers shook her body. The cold had its grip on her. He needed to get her somewhere warm.

He began striding toward the building, toward his old buddy Adrian coming at a run.

Chimera stopped a few yards away, held up his hand, and said, "Hand over the girl, Luke."

"I need to get her warm." Could use a blanket. Maybe two. Didn't they say to combat hypothermia you should get naked and huddle?

"We can help her, but you need to give her to us."

Around him the soldiers held themselves ready. Ready to loose their darts, or would they choose to use bullets? What if they hit Flo? Her body couldn't handle any more. She needed help and arguing or fighting only delayed it.

"Save her." Luke held her out and let the guard with dark skin take Flo from his arms, even as a part of him wanted to howl and fight and never let her go.

He then went to his knees, hands laced behind his head. He knew the drill. He didn't fight as they put him back in his cell.

Not yet.

However, more than ever he knew they had to escape. And soon, before the next monster killed her.

Pacing his room, he wanted to rage and pound and demand an update on Flo.

181

Did she live?

Would she be okay?

He refused to even contemplate her dying. Besides he'd know if she kicked the bucket. He'd feel it.

They'd better hope she didn't die because there would be no stemming his rage.

She was the only thing keeping him sane. The only thing making him want to live.

About three hours after the ill-fated picnic, he heard the locks on his door being pulled. He whirled, fists clenched, ready for anything.

Anything but bad news.

Please, let her be all right.

The door opened, and just one man filled the space, although he could see the movement and shape of others at his back.

"Chimera." He couldn't help the growl and curl of his lip.

"Is that any way to greet me? And to think I came to give you news. Unless you're not curious about the fate of Nurse Henley."

His anger at this man wasn't greater than his need to know. "How is she?"

"Recovering. A lucky thing you were on hand to rescue her. A few moments more in the water, a little longer without air, and we might not be having such a pleasant conversation."

"So she'll be okay?" The relief eased the knot inside him.

"As far as we can tell, she'll not feel any ill side effects, although it will be a few more days before we can say for sure. She was suffering from severe hypothermia, and so we're having to raise her core temperature slowly so as to not shock her system. At the same time, the deep cold permeating her should have prevented any brain damage from the lack of oxygen."

Good news. "I want to see her."

"Is that wise?" Chimera asked. "It's been brought to my attention that you seem unduly attached to the lady."

"Isn't that what you planned?"

Chimera arched a classically shaped brow. "If I did have plans with Nurse Henley, they wouldn't be with you. You might be one of my greatest successes, but you're also far from perfect."

"Don't blow smoke up my ass. We both know you're dying to see if I can make a monster baby."

"You presume to know my mind, and yet you couldn't be more wrong. You're not ready yet."

"Worried my mutated sperm might do something to her?"

"There is nothing wrong with you. And for your information, the genetic changes we accomplished are not transferable."

"Says you."

"If they were, don't you think we'd have exploited that aspect?" Chimera offered him a cold smile.

"Surely you must have realized by now that we've already tried."

"Funny how the body can be willing even when asleep."

The anger burned hot and fierce inside. However, for once, Luke controlled it. "What a surprise, you milked me like a breeding bull. Did you do it yourself, or was Sphincter getting his jollies off doing it?"

"The extraction isn't anything so crude. What is interesting is the lack of motility in your swimmers. It would seem our treatments didn't repair them, as they are quite sluggish and low in number."

A man had his pride, even a prisoner. "Maybe you're not getting a good sample."

"And how exactly do you propose we retrieve it? Is this another hint about using Nurse Henley to slake your lust?"

If only Chimera knew he'd been slaking it every night when he closed his eyes. "You said it yourself, she's attractive."

"She is also an employee of this clinic. We assigned her to you because you showed an interest, and I will admit, under her care you've made excellent strides. However, the reality is Nurse Henley isn't interested in you amorously. And you really shouldn't be thinking of her in those terms, especially since she is only here for a few more months. At the end of her contract, she will move on."

"Whereas I'm a prisoner for life."

"Only if you choose to be. Today was a taste of the freedom you can enjoy again."

"If I agree to be a good boy."

"What are we asking that's so difficult?" Chimera cocked his head.

"I don't want to be a prisoner."

"Very well. What if I moved you to a room where the only lock is one you can engage?"

Luke eyed him, a crease on his brow. "I don't understand."

"You've made great strides. You have your emotions, especially your anger, under control."

"What makes you think that?"

Chimera spread his hands. "You've yet to try and throttle me."

"The temptation is still there." But Luke wasn't dumb. The fleeting pleasure of crushing Chimera's throat wouldn't get him what he wanted.

"You might be tempted, but you're controlling it. Which means I think it's time for you to perhaps become more involved again in the clinic."

"Involved how? Gonna give me a gun and tell me to guard shit again?" Last time he played soldier for the company, he almost put the weapon to his head. It would take only one bullet to stop what Chimera had done.

"We need hunters to help us comb the woods."

"You mean someone with a good sense of smell." Another trait he'd inherited.

"Yes. Someone who can track by scent, sight."

"What am I looking for?"

Chimera's lips flattened. "It would seem the subjects that escaped a while back aren't dead as we first believed."

"Did daddy's experiments come back for a visit?" Luke taunted.

"One of them almost killed Nurse Henley."

"I can't track a lake monster."

"Not that one. The hybrid from the woods. It would be unfortunate if that were to happen again."

"Don't you threaten her." Luke pushed away from the wall he leaned against, body bristling.

Chimera held up a hand. "Not a threat. Just the truth. The creatures are getting bolder, but my men have been unable to take care of them."

"So your plan is to send a monster to catch a monster."

"You are not a monster."

"Aren't I?" Luke said with a sneer.

"Will you do it?"

"Yes. But only a few conditions. One, I want that room you promised. No more guards shadowing my every move."

"Done." The reply was quick.

"And I get to see Margaret. Now."

"She's unconscious."

"Don't care. I see her or there's no deal and you can hope your pet projects don't come back to bite your ass. Literally."

"Very well." Chimera held out his hand.

It was like shaking with the devil. Which was why Luke didn't feel bad that he planned to bolt the first real chance he got.

And fuck anyone who got in his way.

CHAPTER SIXTEEN

MARGARET AWOKE IN A BED.

Not her bed, she should add. She didn't recognize the light suspended overhead. The manacles were also not something she kept in the bedroom. Too kinky for her tastes.

However, she didn't get the impression these were for fun times. Not given the antiseptic smell.

A tug of each arm showed her firmly held, and yet her legs were free. Which didn't do her much good. She didn't have the flexibility to use her toes to untie herself.

"What the hell." She yanked and tugged, panic swamping her quickly at her inability to free herself. Was this how Luke felt when they tied him? Helpless. Afraid. Much easier to understand his anger now that she experienced it.

What she didn't understand was, why had

someone restrained her? Last she recalled she was sinking in water.

Cold. Cold. Water.

She remembered her lungs bursting for air. The need to breathe. The terror as she realized whatever pulled her under wasn't about to set her free.

A sound from behind, the rustle of fabric and the soft scuff of a shoe, did nothing for her panic level.

"Who's there? Where am I?"

"Calm down, Nurse Henley. You're safe," Dr. Chimera said in a soothing tone.

"Untie me at once."

"I intend to. Give me a moment and I'll release you from the restraints." He moved into sight, looking as perfectly coiffed as ever. His deft fingers went to the cuff.

"While you're taking them off, you can explain why I'm tied down in the first place," she snapped. What had happened after she was pulled from the lake?

Who pulled her out?

She recalled a shape arrowing toward her, the eyes glowing green.

Dr. Chimera freed her wrist, and she snatched it close, eyeing him with suspicious caution.

"Nothing nefarious about it. Merely a precaution to ensure you didn't pull the nutrient line from your arm. Surely you've encountered the need before in hospitals with patients who are volatile."

Not often, but it did happen. A turn of her head meant she could see the IV on a pole, the tube extending from it snaking into her arm, the liquid clear. Relief filled her at the lack of color or murk. For a moment she'd feared she was being injected with something else.

"Why are you giving me fluids?" It wasn't standard in drowning cases, given the whole water thing was the problem in the first place.

"We needed to keep you hydrated while you recovered."

"I wasn't out that long." Or so she assumed. No way of telling time in this barren room.

"Longer than you think. The lake water was cold. Too cold for your body to handle. You were suffering from hypothermia. A severe case. It took us the better part of the last four days to regulate your core temperature."

"Four?" It chilled her to realize how much time she'd lost.

"Four and it was iffy for part of it. But thankfully you pulled through."

"Oh." Realizing she'd almost died, her anger deflated. "Thank you."

He finished untying her second wrist and then activated the mechanism to lift the head of the bed. "We weren't about to let you die on us, Nurse Henley. Although, I have to admit, you caused quite the challenge. We've never had someone fall in the lake before and had to improvise when it came to slowly adjusting your core temperature."

Fall? "I didn't fall. Some *thing*"—emphasis on thing—"pulled me in."

"A fish?" A smile hovered around his lips. "I'm pretty sure humans catch the fish and not the other way around."

"I'm telling you something grabbed ahold of me." A slimy tentacle wrapped around her wrist, pulling her hard through the cold water.

"I'm sure it seems very real. However, your recollection is possibly marred by the hypothermia you suffered and the lack of oxygen when you took water into your lungs. Memory loss and false memories can be side effects."

The explanation certainly had some validity, and yet the realism of the memory didn't waver. The details too vivid, too real. The green eyes so bright and somehow familiar. But impossible surely. Which made her wonder. "Who saved me?" Because she'd certainly not saved herself.

"Luke dove in after you."

Luke with vivid orbs that sometimes flashed in her presence. He'd braved freezing cold water to save her? It warmed any cold left in her body. The very idea he'd brave danger to rescue her was the sexiest thing ever. "Did he get hypothermia, too? Is he okay?"

Dr. Chimera retrieved some items from a moving metal tray and laid them on the bed beside her. "Luke is tougher than you when it comes to polar swims. He's fine and enjoying his new quarters. He's been by to see you a few times. You had him quite worried. It would seem you've formed quite the bond."

"We've been nothing but professional," she primly stated.

"Indeed, you have. I've gotten reports on your very perfect patient-nurse interactions." Said in a way that almost sounded mocking. "He's made great strides with your help."

"I didn't really do anything."

"Yet Luke has advanced since he came under your care. He's much calmer now. Cooperative. Cooperative enough he's been moved to the habitat level."

The new surprised her. "He's free?"

"He was never a prisoner, Nurse Henley," Dr. Chimera chided. She noticed how he chose to address her by her title and not her first name. A step back from a month ago when he'd insisted she call him Adrian.

"Since you've deemed him recovered enough to be placed among the staff, does this mean he can leave?"

"Perhaps soon. We want to see how he does first. It wouldn't do to release him too quickly, only to suffer a relapse. Should he continue to make progress, then we'll reevaluate. In the meantime, he has access to the common area and can indulge in outdoor excursions. Under supervision of course. Perhaps you'll join him. Although I might recommend you steer clear of the lake."

She shivered. "Don't go near the lake or the woods. Doesn't leave much. Maybe it would be better to stay inside."

"Now, now, Nurse Henley. Don't let fluke incidents scare you from the beauty of these mountains."

One almost-death experience was a fluke. Two weird occurrences displayed a pattern.

"When can I get out of here?" she asked. Being a patient was for other people. She didn't like the feeling of being an invalid. It made her testy, which again only made her understand Luke more.

Luke. The man who saved her life.

"You may leave as soon as you feel capable," Dr. Chimera replied, spreading his hands.

"I'm ready to go." She swung her legs over the edge of the bed, turning her body, feeling the IV line in her arm tugging.

"Hold on. Let me remove that for you." Chimera leaned close, his fingers, extra hot, deftly pulling free the IV then pressing gauze against the spot.

"I've got it." She shoved at his fingers and applied pressure on the hole to stop any bleeding. The floor swayed underfoot when she hopped off the bed. Her vision spun, and the whole room wobbled for a moment.

Dr. Chimera steadied her with a hand on her arm. "Slowly, Nurse Henley. You've been lying down for quite some time."

"Yeah, so I noticed. I'm fine now." The world had steadied. She felt firmer on her feet. "How long was I out?"

Rather than reply, he said, "Would you like me to escort you to your room?"

"No thanks. I'm sure you have better things to do."

"Ensuring my staff is healthy is important."

She rolled her eyes once she'd stepped past him. What a load of crock. For some reason his words didn't ring true. Perhaps it was Luke's cynicism rubbing off, or Chimera wasn't hiding it as well, but she heard the falseness in his words. Detected even a hint of mockery.

Whatever the case, she wanted away from him.

Lucky for her, she wore socks thick enough to repel the chill of the floor, just like the track suit she wore kept her toasty, especially once she pulled down the sleeves. Exiting, she recognized the location. Her old ward before she took over Luke's care. Level four for patients.

Not saying a word, Chimera followed her, activating the elevator. She wondered for a moment if he would follow her to her room. But he stayed on board when she exited at the habitat level.

Quickly, her strength returning, she made her way to the women's wing and was surprised to see Becky coming out of her room. She almost didn't recognize the girl. The woman seemed hunched in on herself. Frail. If she didn't know better, she'd say Becky appeared afraid.

How long since she'd seen her? Too long she realized. Margaret had gotten too caught up in her work—and burgeoning affair—to notice. "Becky?"

The word sounded loud in the silence, and the girl jumped. As Becky turned to face Margaret, she almost gasped at the sight of her eyes, sunken in her face, her cheeks hollow, her skin sporting a grayish cast.

"What happened to you?"

"I don't know what you mean." Becky pulled the door to her room shut then hugged her sweater more tightly around her body.

"You look exhausted."

"Probably because I am." Shoulders rolled as Becky shrugged. "It happens. I've been working long hours and not sleeping well."

"Is everything okay?"

"I'm fine. Just having some weird nightmares."

"About?" For a moment, she wondered if Becky had formed a bond with someone, too. Someone with less gentle manners.

"I've been dreaming about water. Lots of water with me in it." Becky's lips twisted into a wry smile. "Which is crazy because I don't swim."

"Good thing. That lake is dangerous."

"I heard you fell in and almost drowned."

"I didn't fall." For some reason she blurted it out.

"So, what, someone pushed you?" Becky asked.

Margaret shook her head. "Something in the water yanked me in."

At that, the other woman turned serious. "Do you remember what it looked like?"

It surprised her Becky didn't mock. Chimera certainly hadn't taken her seriously. "I didn't really see it. It felt like a tentacle, though, wrapped around me. But I've never heard of a lake creature with arms. Octopuses live in the oceans." And surely didn't have appendages that long.

"There's all kinds of things in this world we've never discovered. Could be the Ogopogo?"

"The legendary lake monster? It's not real." Margaret wrinkled her nose. She didn't mean to mock, especially since she'd seen the hybrid Sasquatch. But it was too late to temper her remark.

Becky stiffened. "It's possible. The lake is deep and could have something never seen before. Scientists find new species every year."

"Of course, they do. I didn't mean to say it wasn't possible. Dr. Chimera says I imagined it."

"Dr. Chimera says a lot of things. But keep in mind he has secrets."

"That's what Luke says."

"Ah yes, your miracle patient who recovered. I've seen him around. I can see why you didn't mind playing nursemaid." A coy reply.

"I wasn't the one who chose the job," Margaret said, feeling defensive.

"Wonder what they'll have you doing now that he's all better."

Now that Becky mentioned it, she wondered herself. "I'm sure they'll find me something to do."

"Speaking of doing, I should get back to work."

"Take care of yourself, Becky. You really do look run-down. Maybe you should ask for some time off."

At Margaret's words, meant to be caring about her friend, Becky shook off the slumping shoulders and wan expression. "I don't need a break." Becky shook her head, and her eyes took on an angry cast. "What? So you can take my place? I don't think so."

Not really, given how bad Becky looked. "I'm worried about you is all. Maybe you should see about getting some vitamins or something. Have you been getting fresh air?"

"I don't need you worrying about me," the once bubbly girl snapped. "I'm fine. All good. I just came to grab a sweater. I'm going for a walk."

"Do you want me to come with you?"

The glare said it all.

She stared at Becky's back, stunned by the change, but at the same time unsure what she could do about it.

Entering her room, she found herself restless. Unable to sit still. It didn't help that her terminal was down. She wanted to see Luke. Especially since she didn't remember dreaming of him at all during her recovery. Had her almost drowning broken the link between them?

I have to see him.

But how? Chimera said Luke had been moved to a new room. How would it look if she asked someone to tell her where? Nothing wrong with a nurse inquiring about a patient. Especially the man who'd saved her.

That was the argument she used to convince herself. She'd find someone and ask them to point her in Luke's direction.

Before leaving her room, she took a moment to shower, needing to wash the smell of the antiseptic ward from her skin. Whilst in the shower, she spent a moment checking herself over. Turned her wrist back and forth. The skin appeared smooth and unblemished.

The only mark was the one on her arm from the IV, barely a red pinprick. No bruising. No mottled skin from the hypothermia. No sign she'd almost died at all.

She dressed comfortably and pulled her hair back into a ponytail, and then she went in search of her dream lover.

Four days she'd slept. Four days and she didn't recall a single thing from it. Had they induced a coma? She'd not thought to ask Dr. Chimera, and yet that seemed to be the case, else she'd have regained consciousness here and there.

A coma would explain the lack of dreamtime. Because she refused to contemplate a possibility that the link between her and Luke was broken.

He saved me. Surely that strengthened the bond.

Odd how she didn't have a problem believing they share an esoteric link but scoffed at the idea of a lake monster.

What were the chances of two legendary creatures in one place?

If she listened to Luke, it wasn't coincidence but science.

Science gone wrong.

The hallway for the women's wing ended at the intersection, and she halted as she found the object of her thoughts coming out of the men's wing.

At the sight of her, Luke's nostrils flared and his eyes flashed.

Green fire in them. There one minute, gone the next. Just like in the water. What did it mean?

Is he a monster, too?

She didn't let the idea take root as he exclaimed, "Flo!" His expression was bright with surprise and happiness. Luke took long strides toward her. Ignoring the camera surely watching, he scooped her into his arms and hugged her tight. He buried his face in her hair and whispered, "I was so worried."

"I'm fine." At least she seemed to be on the surface, but her mind was a different matter. Confusion plagued her, and she didn't know a cure for it. Although, the press of his body, his real body for once, not the dream one, did alleviate some of her concern.

Still whispering he said, "I couldn't find you in my dreams."

"I know." She pulled away lest those watching make note of their inappropriate intimacy. "I hear I should thank you for saving me."

"No thanks. I should have paid better attention."

He blamed himself for what happened? "Not your fault I'm clumsy."

"You almost died."

The reminder caused her heart to stutter. "But I didn't. I'm fine now. Although I am beginning to wonder at my luck. That's twice now the wildlife in this place has almost killed me. Did you see what grabbed me?" He'd surely know what it was.

Luke hesitated before saying. "What do you mean grabbed? You fell in."

Lie.

She wondered if the cameras watching heard the falseness in his words. The damned cameras. Always spying and listening.

She wanted away from this place.

Away from it all.

The only problem was she didn't want to leave without Luke. And now that he was deemed well enough to come and go from the clinic at his discretion, the possibility for them being together away from here was possible.

Just one problem. How could she discuss it with him? What if the dreams were done? She needed a way to speak with him. A way that wouldn't be overheard.

Only one place didn't have cameras. "Despite the disaster of our last one, I think we should go on another picnic."

"Ready to get back on that picnic horse?" His lips curved. "When? Now? I'm free."

The temptation to say yes was there; however, given the lethargy pulling at her, she wasn't sure she could make it that far. "Not right this second. I know I slept for a few days, but I am exhausted. Tomorrow? Maybe we could take a walk around the track."

"Sounds like a plan. After a few days lying around like a sack of potatoes, you are in dire need of some cardio."

"Potatoes?" was her dry reply. "So you think I'm lumpy?

He laughed. "Are you fishing for compliments, Flo?"

"Of course not."

"In case you are, then you should know you are the sexiest nurse I know even when you're passed out and drooling."

"I did not drool."

His lips quirked. "Only a little. It was the snoring that was jarring."

She hit him in the arm. "I do not snore."

The laughter proved loud and contagious. Her lips curved into a smile.

"I see you're feeling better. Back to beating me."

"I did not," she huffed. Then added a slyer, "Pussy."

He grabbed his heart. "Did you just call my manhood into question?"

At his light banter, she giggled. This Luke reminded her of dream Luke, the more relaxed one. It was nice to see him acting the same way in the real world.

He truly was getting better.

A yawn caused her jaw to crack, and her cheeks heated in embarrassment. "I'm sorry."

"No, I am. You're tired, and I'm yapping your ear off. Let me escort you to your room."

"You can't. Men aren't..." She never did finish the sentence. Her words trailed off as Luke placed a hand in the middle of her back and propelled her down the hall. "I don't understand. How come the alarm didn't go off?"

Luke snickered. "Because I filched Sphinx's card this morning." He held it up and twirled it.

"Why would you do that?" she exclaimed.

"Shits and giggles."

"You're going to get in trouble." She tried to halt her steps and turn around, but Luke kept her moving.

"Don't worry, Flo. It's just a prank. No big deal."

"But what if they get mad? They might put you back on level six." Lock him away, and then how would they leave?

"Everything is going to be all right. I'm doing much better, and I had a talk with the big guy."

"You prayed to God?"

At that, Luke barked a laugh. "No. I don't pray. Jeezus, the very idea is ludicrous. I meant I talked to Chimera. Told him I'd be a good boy and do whatever I was told."

"Taking someone's keycard isn't doing as you're told," she scolded.

"Don't be such a worry wart. Is this your room?" he asked as she halted in front of her door.

"Yeah. Thanks for walking me." She suddenly realized she didn't have a card to get in. "Shoot." She'd have to go find someone to give her a new one.

"Hold on." He slapped the card on her reader. Given Sphinx had access to this hall, she half expected it to work.

It didn't. The intercom however did crackle. "Unauthorized entry."

"Hello. Is someone listening? I can't get into my room," she said aloud.

"State your name and position."

"Margaret Henley. I'm a nurse on level six."

"Voice match found." The door slid open.

"Thank you." Said more in relief than anything else.

As she stepped over the threshold, she turned to say good-bye, only to move back as Luke crowded her coming in, his expression determined. For some reason this made her nervous.

She watched him, wringing her hands, not understanding why she felt a little off kilter. This was the Luke from her dreams. The man she'd lain with. She knew every inch of his body.

In her dreams.

In the real world, he was so much more imposing. So much more *there*.

"I'm fine. You can go now. I'll see you later. Tomorrow," she said quickly in correction.

He pulled back the sheets on her bed before turning to look at her. He blew out a breath. "Flo. You look like a doe caught in front of the wolf. I ain't gonna hurt you."

"I know. It's just..." She paused and licked her lips. "Do you realize this is the first time we've ever been alone with no cameras or anybody watching?"

"First time we've been within reach of a bed, too." He arched a brow.

Heat pooled between her legs.

"We really shouldn't." A weak statement that she didn't mean at all given she took a step toward him.

"You're right, we shouldn't." He tugged her into his arms, a quick embrace that then involved him shoving her toward the bed. "You need to rest. You look like shit."

"Um, thanks?" She wrinkled her nose.

Luke laughed. "Actually, you look delicious and tempting. Too tempting. Which is why I have to leave, or you won't get any sleep."

"Is that such a bad thing?" Look at her with her wanton words.

"Yes, because I've actually got a job to do."

"Job?"

"Part of the conditions of my release." He rolled his eyes.

Her lips pulled into a wide smile. "That's great, Luke. See, I told you things would get better."

"They will." He leaned down and kissed her on the forehead and whispered, "I promise. See you later in our dreams."

"You think..." She raised her gaze. "What if..." She couldn't say it.

"We're still connected, you and I. So don't worry, Flo. We'll talk tonight. Get some rest."

Another light kiss, and then he left. But she didn't

have time to lament his absence as fatigue tugged her down.

Down...

She dreamed, but it wasn't the nice dreams with Luke and pleasure. This was a nightmare, full of darkness and shadows. Of her running in the woods, frightened. Chased.

And when she fell, she was surrounded, the glowing eyes of predators ringing her. Drawing closer.

Hungry.

So...hungry. The green pair hungriest of all. And when they neared, she saw the monstrous face, the slavering mouth with all its teeth.

All the better to eat you with.

Chomp.

"Aaaaah!" As the nightmare closed its jaws on her, she sat bolt upright in bed, soaked in sweat, her heart pounding. The terror still holding her in its grip.

It took a moment to realize she was alone and unharmed. No monsters in her bedroom. No eyes watching.

It was only a nightmare. Not what she'd hoped for when she lay her head down. Then again, given she was napping at three in the afternoon, she couldn't expect Luke to be napping, too.

Getting to her feet, she found herself feeling much better. The lethargy of before mostly gone. But her tummy did rumble. A glance at her watch showed the hour late. She'd slept through dinner, but there were the machines in the hall with edible offerings.

Heading to her door, she opened it and almost stepped on something in the way. A tray sat on the floor, a silver dome on it, along with a bottle of water infused with electrolytes. Bringing the tray into her room, she set it down on her desk and noticed the note tucked under the bottle.

Thought you could use something warm and filling. I'm just outside pulling guard duty if you want to come find me. Luke.

The fact he'd thought of her warmed Margaret to her toes.

Hungry and eager, she ate the bowl of soup under the dome. It wasn't scorching hot, but still warm enough to fill her belly. The water proved tangy, the lemon flavoring not exactly her thing.

Fed, she thought about going to bed again. After all, it was close to her usual bedtime. However, she didn't feel tired, and the note did mention that Luke was outside.

Doing what? Was this about the job Chimera gave him?

It surprised her the amount of freedom they gave Luke. Sure, she'd told him to be patient, that it would come; however, he'd gone from six guards to escort him outside to wandering at will.

She should be happy for him. However, suspicion made her wonder at the sudden change in heart. Why didn't she trust his newfound freedom?

Because...

Because something strange was happening at the

Chimaeram Clinic. Starting with why she remained passed out for four days? Hypothermia, and the treatment of it, didn't take that long. Why all the lies about her falling in? Why not admit there was something in the lake?

Then there was the pink barrette. Wild animals didn't do their hair.

What if Luke was telling the truth? What if Dr. Chimera did have secrets and the clinic truly was doing something heinous, like experimenting on people? It seemed farfetched, the kind of thing that only happened in a horror movie, and yet, once upon a time, things like cell phones and the internet appeared impossible, too.

Science kept advancing, and there were those who didn't abide by the rules and ethics set in place. Those who might be tempted to play God with genetics and other things.

It would sure as hell explain the thing from the woods. Hybrid Sasquatch and wolf, ha! The more she thought about it, the less sense it made. Experiments on humans would explain why Luke kept claiming he was a monster. Did he fear becoming like that wild creature?

Surely not, and how could she even contemplate it? Luke wasn't an animal. He was a man. A man she cared for.

Maybe even loved.

The latter had her blinking. Had she done the unthinkable and fallen for her patient?

Then again, in their dreams, he wasn't broken or in need of her help. He was strong and loving and gentle.

She fell in love with *that* man.

A man she needed to see. She wrapped herself in a sweater before heading aboveground. Trepidation filled her at the thought of going outside, especially at night. It was dangerous.

But Luke was up there. She felt safe with him. Besides, she wouldn't go far.

The elevator spilled her onto the main floor, empty of people this time of night. Her keycard, which she'd found on the tray along with her meal, gave her access to the outside, which wasn't as dark as expected.

Light pooled from two caged bulbs, their incandescent illumination holding back the shadows.

Yet their glow didn't show Luke nearby. No one appeared to be outside. No one at all.

Was he perhaps on the rooftop? He'd not specified where he'd be in his note.

A few paces took her away from the building with her keeping a wary gaze on the shadows just past the farthest border of light. She craned upwards but couldn't really see the upper edge of the roofline. Another a half-dozen steps put her closer to the darkness than the door. She stood on concrete still, and the woods were yards and yards away.

Glancing upward, she couldn't see anyone standing atop the building.

"Luke?" She said his name softly.

No reply.

"Luke." She stated it louder, more firmly. Determined to leave if he didn't answer. She wondered if his note meant he'd been outside earlier. She had no way of knowing what time he left it.

For all she knew, he was in his room going to sleep, looking for her in a dream.

This is crazy. She was about to move back to the safety of indoors when she heard it.

A soft whisper on the evening breeze. *"Helloooooo."*

It didn't come from the building.

Turning, she frowned at the darkness beyond the circle of light.

"Luke? Is that you?"

"Luke is that you?" The words echoed back, the voice feminine. Lilting. Mocking.

Fear iced her veins. Not again. Rather than wait and see who spoke, Margaret ran for the door, only to halt and almost stumble as a figure darted into the pool of light, gangly and grinning through a mess of hair.

Much like the hybrid she'd met before, the body was human in appearance—two arms, two legs—but upright rather than on all fours. The face was where her mind had problems adjusting because the nose was all wrong, as was the jaw. But the eyes, the glowing yellow eyes, were all too human, as was the kinky blonde hair. As to the rest of the body, the smock pants and shirt were identical to those the patients wore—just dirtier.

"Who are you?" Margaret asked even as she was tempted to ask, *What are you?*

"Who are you?" the creature mimicked.

"I'm Margaret." She pointed to her chest, hoping the aping was a sign of intelligence. She also hoped by stalling someone would notice and come to her rescue.

"I'm..." The head cocked. "Jennnnnnnnnny." The creature held the consonant in her name almost singing it. Then giggled. But it was the growl that raised all the hairs on Margaret's body.

"Hi, Jenny. Do you live around here?" How much did this creature understand? It seemed very odd to her that she'd now run into two possible Sasquatches when the Bigfoot hunters of this world couldn't locate one.

"Hungry." Jenny took a step forward.

"You need food? I can get you food. I just need to go inside to get some."

"Hungry," Jenny repeat, taking more strides toward Margaret, her eyes shining brightly as if lit from within. Her jaw unlocked, opening a mouth too wide with teeth too plenty.

"I'll get you food. I swear." Margaret began to back away, stepping from the false safety of light into the shadows beyond.

"Hungry." A word said with a lilt and a giggle.

Whereas Margaret let out a scream as arms wrapped around her from behind!

CHAPTER SEVENTEEN

THE SHARP, FEMININE CRY CUT OFF, SENDING A chill through Luke. It sounded like Margaret, which was impossible. She was inside. Asleep. Even if she had woken, surely she wouldn't venture outside, especially not at night.

Whether it was Margaret or not, he had to investigate. He jogged around the building—Chimera's pet soldiers following. For the past few days they'd been hunting for escaped projects.

That was what the doctors called them. "Projects" or by their assigned designation. For example, Luke was WF007. There were many abbreviations and numbers in use, mostly because the early experiments had failed.

But the clinic always found stupidly willing people. People, like Luke, at the end of their rope, looking for a miracle. And he'd found one. However, Luke remained cognizant of the fact he was one of the lucky ones. Not all the recipients of Chimera's treatments recovered as well. Like Luke, they resented what was done to them, and revenge was never far from their thoughts. But above their need to spill the blood of those who wronged them was their desire to be free.

A batch of projects escaped awhile back. Having been put in solitary by then, Luke only heard the rumors. How the changed ones fled to the mountains. Nine in that specific breakout. Although it was possible more had fled Chimera's tight grip since then.

Luke secretly cheered them on. It seemed the changed ones didn't go too far and had lost what humanity they had left. Everyone thought them long gone. Either fled or dead. Until a few months ago. That was when the first person went missing. A nurse who enjoyed walks in the woods.

All they ever found was a shoe.

The next victim, an orderly this time, left behind a finger and a pool of blood.

That was when the already tight security got tighter. Not inside the clinic, but outside.

It seemed Chimera's pet projects had returned, and they were out for blood. Which, in turn, made all the doctors nervous. Hardly anyone went outside, and those that did were armed to the teeth.

This fear was why Chimera wanted Luke to track them. Personally, he didn't want to find them. Let them eke out whatever existence they could. They'd been tortured enough already. However, in the guise of playing along, he pretended each day to go looking for them. And when he turned up empty-handed, agreed to do a hunt at night.

His last hunt he'd decided because now that Margaret was awake, it was time for them to flee.

A plan that would have to wait again because as he rounded the side of the building, the odors and their story hit him hard and fast.

First, the scent of the creature he'd dubbed, Doe. She'd been lurking around in the woods, watching out of sight. He caught the more fetid stench of the male who'd left behind the carcass of a deer in the woods, less than half a mile from the clinic. He called him Stinky.

More worrisome, mingled with both those odors, was the delicate aroma of Flo. His woman.

She'd come outside.

He followed the scents from the open area ringing the doorway until it moved off into the shadows.

She was gone.

Taken.

Heart pounding, Luke turned to scan the darkness, seeing more shapes and nuances in the shadows than a mere human could. But he saw no sign of Margaret.

He lifted his nose and sniffed, swiveling his head left and right to truly get a feel for the direction the scents went.

There. To his left.

With need driving him, he didn't let the beast within slumber. He called it forth. Called on the adrenaline that took his humanity and turned him into a monster.

A hunter. Because that was what Chimera originally tried to design. Someone with better olfactory senses than a human. Improved eyesight. And the inborn instinct of a predator.

A killer.

No longer would Luke let the lost souls roaming these hills live. They'd taken his Flo.

My female.

Mine.

"Mine..." A softly growled word.

How dare they! For their transgression, they would die. And if they hurt her, they'd die painfully.

He chuffed as he loped past the civilized areas toward the wild forest, eager to enter the sheltering boughs, to inhale the scent of life and death. A place that felt like home.

A part of him realized his thoughts were not rational. Not *human*. He didn't care.

Only one driving need had him racing toward the woods, ignoring the shouts of the soldiers behind him. His woman needed him, and he found the strength to increase his gait. The others, impeded by their humanity, couldn't keep pace. At least they didn't shoot him as he ran ahead. Their yells weren't of panic because he ran.

Not even close. They were excited. They, too, felt the lure of the hunt. The thrill of the chase.

Tossing his head back, he uttered a long howl, a

deep and resonant sound that lifted into the night and gave warning that he was coming.

I will find you.

And you will die.

As he crossed the edge of the woods, the very life within it enveloped him. It had a scent. Leaves—some growing, others decaying on the ground—fragrant and distinct. The odor of green growing things and mildewing bark. Of squirrel musk and chipmunk nuts. Even the fungi that took root in the damp pockets.

And twining through all those smells, his quarry. And Flo.

The scents drew him onward, and he barked in warning. Let them know he came. Let them bow before his might.

Sprinting through the tree trunks, he lost the soldiers. They had to go slower, hampered by their shitty night vision. They lacked his sure footedness, his instinct. His skill.

For once he didn't fight the beast within. He embraced it. Encouraged it to come because he'd need the strength.

He weaved through the wooden sentinels, breath chuffing hotly through his nostrils, his blood pounding through his veins, pumping his muscles. He neared his prey, and excitement had him showing teeth. Teeth that ached in his gums.

He caught up to his targets in a small clearing, wide enough for the moon's rays to penetrate, lighting the space in an eerie silver light. He paused on the edge and lifted his head, uttering a challenging howl.

In reply, the male he hunted, body hunched, tusks projecting from his cheeks, dropped his burden.

Nay, not a burden, but his female, who cried out as she hit the ground.

It was enough to send Luke barreling across the clearing in a rage.

He rammed into the other, and they hit the ground hard. Rolling and scrabbling. Fingers tipped in claws tearing for purchase. Tearing. Straining. Mouths snapping.

He had to watch the sharp tusks of the male he fought. Avoid their tearing points.

The thing—Stinky, his mind reminded—fought rabidly and without finesse, giving Luke an edge. He knew his teeth and claws weren't the only things he could use to his advantage. Fight smart.

Words that someone once spoke to him and that he remembered. But he had no tools.

A blow from the side sent him staggering, the woman, getting involved, and much as it bothered him to hit a female, he had no choice but to shove her when she ran at him screaming.

It however distracted him from the real problem. Stinky rammed into him, driving him back until he hit a tree trunk. Hard. His head snapped back, and he bit his tongue. Which only served to make him angrier.

"Enough already," he roared. Adrenaline coursed inside him, and he shoved at the beastman, his muscles pumped. He began to swing, ham-fisted, striking Stinky with meaty thuds. Over and over, pummeling him into retreat.

But the woman had time to recover. She threw herself around his knees, sending him toppling. Stinky took advantage and popped on top. Snarling, slobbering, and genuinely being gross.

Twisting, Luke managed to roll them so he pinned Stinky with his knees. Bone crunched as he pressed all his weight. He managed to manacle Stinky's wrists, leaving him squirming and hissing under him.

Kill him.

The imperative filled him, and he pressed harder, ignoring the whimpers of the female who watched. His lip curled over his teeth, and he glared in triumph at the enemy beneath him.

Die.

The gaze of the beast met his. Eyes that were suddenly calm with acceptance. Even relief.

In that moment, the man within remembered this wasn't a creature under him but a victim. A brother of science.

"No." He tried to reason with the thing, his words guttural and rough. "No fight."

He never had a chance to find out if he could reason with Stinky. A blow to the back of his head knocked him off the other male. The treachery had him rolling and snarling even as blood poured hotly into his eyes. Stinky's mate had come to his rescue, the whimpering but an act.

No more weakness. No mercy. He snapped and took a step forward, a low growl rumbling. A raised fist was all it took. The female cowered then dropped to her knees, head bowed in submission.

"Why?" he snarled. But he knew that answer. The roiling darkness inside them. The animal instinct to guard. To dominate.

Except, in a pack of animals, there could be only one leader.

When Stinky moved, he didn't look but felt his foot connect. *Crack*. The female gasped.

And yet the other man still wanted to fight. Rose to his knees, blood dripping from his jaw to growl a challenge.

The sound that rumbled from Luke had no word. Yet it rang with demand; *submit*.

Stinky lifted his chin, only to flinch as the female cuffed him and then purred a sound. Chastised, the male rolled to his knees and hung his head.

Defeated. Submissive to the alpha.

Me.

Luke lifted his head to the sky and howled.

He'd won. He'd prevailed and brought the enemy to his knees. He'd saved his female. He turned his gaze on her and smiled.

Wide eyes met his glance. Her lips parted. In awe. Respect. She uttered a feminine sound, "Eep!"

Then, to reward his prowess, his mate chose to play and bolted into the woods.

CHAPTER EIGHTEEN

Ohmygod. Ohmygod.

Margaret's breathing heaved and huffed, whistling with panic as she ran for dear life away from the monsters in the clearing.

Yes, monsters. The ones who captured her and the one who came to her rescue.

Or did he come for something else? Hard to tell with that savage light in *its* eyes. The fierce snarl on *its* face.

Terror had her running as they fought. Away from it all.

Her panic-driven steps took her deeper into the woods. She lost all sense of direction and had no idea where she was.

Not that she had any idea before her flight. When the smelly thing took her, he dumped her upside down over his shoulder and then loped away, the jostle enough to make her nauseous. It didn't help her addled brain when she got dumped on the hard ground. Her disorientation as she blinked at the thing that challenged it.

The thing with green eyes.

She couldn't think of it. Didn't want to remember what came to her aid.

Who...

It couldn't be. All those times he'd claimed he was a monster, she'd said no. He didn't look like a monster. Didn't act like one. Until he arrived in that clearing.

In shape, he was still Luke, tall and broad, wearing the same sweatshirt and pants as before. But his face...

His features had a sharper cast to them, more lupine in nature, wicked, too. His teeth glinted in the moonlight, and his eyes glowed.

Glowed motherfucking green.

Which was why, when Luke engaged the other creature in battle, she took off running.

He is *a monster*.

She'd not believed. She'd thought him delusional, and all along he told the truth. She couldn't handle it. Feared it.

Feared him.

Branches whipped her skin as she ran. But the pain of them wasn't why she cried. Terror accounted for part of it, but mostly it was heartache.

I loved him. Past tense, because how could she love a...a...wolfman. Because that was how he seemed and how he sounded when he uttered that chilling howl.

She couldn't hear any sounds of fighting behind

her. She could hear nothing at all but her own harsh pants as she ran. Ran to where? There was nowhere safe.

If the monsters didn't get her, the exposure in the woods would. Even if she did find her way back to the clinic, she was no safer. She had seen their secret. Chimera would never let her leave. She knew too much.

Would he lock her away like he had Luke? Would he experiment on her, as well? Put her in a coma like those other patients that he might inject her with mad-science concoctions?

Would—

"Aaahh." Her sharp scream cut through the night as arms lifted her from the ground. She thrashed and kicked.

A voice tried to soothe. "Flo, it's all right. It's me. You're safe."

"Let me go. You—you—monster!"

The word saw his grip loosen, and she pulled away from Luke, only to whirl that she might keep him in sight.

There was scant moonlight here, and yet she saw enough.

Saw the fading glow in his eyes, the sad curve of his lips. The rounded defeat in his shoulders.

And she felt shame.

"Luke, I'm sorry." She reached out, only he flinched and her chagrin deepened.

"Sorry for what?" was his bitter retort. "Telling the truth? I am a monster, Flo. I tried to tell you."

"And I didn't believe," she said. "I'm sorry. I should have listened."

He wouldn't look at her. "I'm kind of glad you didn't. It was nice to feel almost normal for a while."

Saying she was sorry again wouldn't cut it. Couldn't fix the hurt she heard in his words. "What are you, exactly?"

"A mish-mash of DNA from all kinds of creatures. But the dominant gene seems to be wolf."

"You're a wolfman." It sounded crazy to say it aloud.

"Yes."

"A killer."

He snorted. "Only if threatened."

"Are you feeling threatened?"

His nostrils flared, and he shot her a glare. "Are you asking if I'm going to hurt you? Because the answer is no. I would never fucking hurt you. I came out here to save you."

"Thank you." A trite reply for what he'd done. "What happens now?"

"To me or you?"

"Both. I know your secret."

"You could pretend you don't. Fake it well enough and Chimera might even believe you."

"But you don't think he'll let me go."

He shrugged. "I don't really know."

"What about you? Are you going to run before they catch up?"

"Is there any point? What do I have to look forward to, Flo? You said it, I'm a monster. Where is there for me to go?"

The defeat in him hurt. Hurt because she knew she was the cause. And why did she fear him?

Someone had changed him, not by his choice. Yes, it was damned scary. Yet at the same time, he was still the man she loved. A man who never lied about what had happened to him. A man who never hurt her.

"Why did you come after me?"

"Why do you think?" he snapped. "I care for you, Flo. I wasn't about to let that monster have you."

She took a step forward. "How do I know I can trust you?"

"You can't." The words emerged blunt and gruff. "I'm not human anymore. Sometimes I feel more beast than man. I should have never gotten involved with you."

"Then why did you?"

"At first, I thought the dreams weren't real."

"And after?"

He shrugged. "I couldn't resist you."

The stark honesty in his words hit her. As did what she knew about him. He'd never hurt her. On the contrary, twice he'd risked himself to save her.

She trusted him more than she trusted pretty much everyone else in her life. So why was she pushing him away?

She closed the gap between them. He tried to turn his face when she went to cup his cheeks. She wouldn't let him escape. She grabbed him. Forced him to face her. Met his green gaze with her own.

"I love you, Luke Harris. Even if you are the wolfman."

"You don't know what you're saying."

"I'm saying I accept you for you who are. Remember what you asked me in the dream?"

"It was wrong. I can't ask you to run with me. It's not a life. I won't do it to you." He shook his head, breaking free of her touch, and she knew he lied.

"Don't I get a choice?" She gripped him again, stared at him until he met her gaze. Until she could see the longing. The hope tempered with defeat. He thought he didn't deserve her. He was oh so wrong. "I love you. And if we have to hide to be together, then we hide. As far as it takes to keep you away from Chimera and his clinic."

"Running away means leaving everything behind," Luke reminded her.

"I have nothing that means more to me right now than you."

"I might go crazy yet, like those lost souls in the woods." His true fear emerged in those tight words, and yet she didn't let them scare her.

"I won't let you." She'd find a way to keep him sane. To keep his primal urges at bay.

"If we go, it has to be now. We won't get another chance," he said, turning his head to peer behind him.

"Then I guess we go, but where to? And how?"

"Out of these mountains and on foot, I guess."

"But it's so far." She chewed her lip, daunted by the idea.

"Would you rather return to the clinic?"

Back to a place that might put her in a locked room with no escape? She shook her head. "Let's go." Now, before she changed her mind and thought about the folly of it.

Linking fingers, they began walking through the woods, Luke's pace brisk. The pressing weight of the darkness and strange forest made her babble.

"Thanks for the soup. Glad I ate it before coming to find you."

"What soup?"

"The one you left outside my door with the note..." Her voice trailed off. "You didn't leave the tray, did you? Or that note telling me to meet you outside."

"Like fuck I did. There are monsters in the woods. I would have never told you to come out at night. But that means someone did." His expression hardened. "Chimera."

"But why?"

"Who the fuck knows why. Sick fuck. He's planning something."

"Planning what?"

He didn't reply, instead cocked his head.

"What's wrong?" she asked.

"Engines. Probably some guards on ATVs."

"What do we do?" Because they couldn't outrun machines.

"Hide. Now," he barked, shoving her toward a shadowy hump. "There's a log there. Duck behind it and cover yourself in leaves."

"What about you?"

"I can handle myself if you're not there distracting me."

She snared him by the shirt and hauled him close. "Don't you dare die on me now." She pressed a hard kiss against his lips, feeling his chuckle vibrating.

"I don't intend to die. Now hide, Flo. Before they see you."

She scurried to conceal herself, her heart racing again, her nose tickling as she ducked behind the moldy log. But she didn't bury herself in leaves. She glanced over the edge and saw Luke standing there, waiting.

Waiting for what?

The roar of a motor grew louder, and a light pierced the shadows split in streams by the trees in its path. Rather than conceal himself, Luke held his hands by his side and slightly crouched. Surely, he didn't plan to fight?

As the ATV burst into view, he moved. Jumping into the air and somehow landing on the driver. The two went tumbling to the ground, out of sight, and the ATV kept going, coming right at her. She ducked behind the log and flinched as the vehicle hit it. Then stopped.

Its dual headlights shone past her and blinded her to what happened. But she could hear.

Hear the growling. Bestial and fierce.

The guard cursing, "Fucking monster. I'm going to blow your head off."

The sickening crunch.

And then nothing.

She peeked over the edge of the log, her hand curled around a rock she found. At first, she saw nothing. A shadow moved into view, standing in front of her.

The combat gear not Luke's.

The voice said, "On your knees, or I'll shoot." Terrifying even if not directed at her.

Around the bulky shape, she saw Luke appear, his eyes glowing frightfully bright. His hands laced over his head.

"I'm obeying," said Luke. "See. Dropping to my knees. No need to be trigger-happy."

"You killed Burton." A statement that Luke didn't deny.

"I did."

"Fucking monster." The guard held the gun to Luke's head, and she closed her eyes to what happened next.

CHAPTER NINETEEN

Luke stared in disbelief at Margaret, who still held the rock in her hand. The soldier lay crumpled at her feet.

She'd saved him.

Saved the monster, in more ways than she might realize. Now to save her.

He stood quickly. "We need to go."

She blinked.

"Flo?"

She dropped the rock, her eyes wide with shock.

"Flo..." Said more softly. "We have to leave now. If you still want to."

His words snapped her out of the staring daze. She nodded.

First thing, he wrenched the headlights off the front of the four-wheeler. Then took care of the taillights. No use making them into a target.

When he was done, he found Flo holding a gun by

the barrel, offering him the butt. "We should probably take this," she said softly.

"Good thinking. He tucked the gun in his waistband. "Climb on." He straddled the ATV and waited for her to perch behind him, her arms locked around his waist, before he took off. He hated the loudness of the engine, but loved how it ate up the terrain, taking them farther and faster than they could have on foot.

They managed to go miles into the mountains, far enough that the distant helicopter searching never caught their track. Far and long enough that they ran out of gas and ditched the vehicle to keep moving on foot.

They went until he knew she could go no farther, and then he carried her, amazed at the fact she'd chosen him. Chosen him despite the fact he was a monster.

A part of him chastised himself for even asking her to run. What was he thinking, asking a nurse, a gorgeous one at that, to love a wolfman? He probably wasn't being fair. Certainly not to her. He was taking her from everything she knew. Everything she was.

Yet, for all the danger and uncertainty, he'd never been happier.

She chose me.

And he chose her.

I love you, Flo. He'd protect her with his dying breath. Or walk for hours while she slept in his arms, and when she woke, they walked even farther until night fell again. But by the time the stars emerged, they were ensconced in a cave, long abandoned by whatever used it as a den in the past. A perfect spot to pile up some leaves. With the dark and cloudy night, and the cave so deep, he even dared to build a fire, the crevice at the back of the cave forming the perfect chimney.

In their den, they snuggled, Flo sitting between his legs, her head against his shoulder.

"Are you okay?" he asked when she sighed.

"Surprisingly, yes. You never told me you knew how to live off the land." Referring to the rabbit he'd snared and cooked, the foliage he'd scavenged that was safe to eat.

"I know how to survive." More than ever, he'd need those skills.

"Do you think we can really make it out of the mountains?"

"Yes." He didn't mention how long it might take, though, or how treacherous parts of it might be. And that wasn't even adding in the fact Chimera would have his men looking for them.

"Can I ask you something?"

"Anything, Flo."

"Why? Why did he do that to you?"

"Because I said yes."

She shifted and frowned at him. "You asked to become a wolfman?"

He laughed. "Yes and no. I asked for a cure and didn't care if there were any side effects. I was tired of the pain. Of feeling less than a man."

"Being disabled doesn't make you less manly."

"An easy thing to say when you're not living it day by day. Remembering how it felt to run and longing for an end to the pain. There wasn't a combination of drugs and booze that could truly make me forget it was there. So when Chimera gave me a chance, I took it."

"The treatment..." She paused as if to find the right words. "It changed you."

"It did. And before you ask, I'm not sure how it works."

"He gave you wolf genes."

"He did. Still don't know why wolf instead of something else. I mean wolves aren't close to humans at all. So what made him choose them for the treatment?" He shrugged. "Wolf isn't even the only thing he used. It's just what's dominant inside me," he said, remembering only the elation when he realized his body was whole again. "I didn't even know there was something wrong until something made me mad and I growled that first time." A deep low sound that frightened him.

"He found a way to make a legend true."

"You mean make me a werewolf?" He chuckled. "Not exactly. I don't completely change into a beast, although once my adrenaline gets going, I can get hairier and toothier."

"Your eyes glow, too."

"Yeah, I'm a fucking jack-o-lantern. Which weird because wolves in the wild don't glow in the dark. I'm pretty sure there's more to the whole splicing thing than wolf DNA. Even after Chimera fixed me, he kept tinkering. I think he was trying to figure out why I stayed sane when so many others didn't."

"Those things in the woods..."

"Once people. Victims like me. They also got the treatments but didn't do as well as I did. Many of the people Chimera treats die."

"I'm glad you didn't die."

"Funny thing is, since meeting you, I'm glad I didn't either." He kissed her on the temple. "You've given me hope, Flo." Even as he was more terrified than ever. What if his body and mind failed him? What if he turned into a mindless beast? Would he know enough in time to make sure he couldn't harm Flo?

"And you make me feel alive." She turned in his arms and straddled him.

"I'm afraid, though, Flo. What if..." He couldn't say it.

She said it for him. "What if you turn primal?" She shook her head. "Not going to happen. I won't let it. We'll fight this. Together." She snaked an arm around his neck and pulled him close for a kiss. A soft kiss that aroused every one of his senses, especially since it was their first real one. The one in his cell didn't count because he was proving a point. The dream ones just weren't the same.

This, though... This melding of lips caused a heat that left her breathless.

She pulled away, cheeks flushed. "I guess it's not a good time to be doing that."

"I think we're fine for a bit," he murmured against

her mouth. He deepened the kiss, demanding more, caressing her and imprinting her feel and taste. Her lips parted, granting his tongue access. He slid it along hers, and when she returned the favor, he sucked it. She rocked on his lap, the core of her pressing on him, the scent of her making him dizzy with desire.

Their clothing dared get in the way of what he needed. Skin-to-skin contact.

"You're wearing too many clothes," he grumbled.

"We can't have that, now can we?" she said with a laugh. Flo aided him in peeling the shirt from his back, and he made quick work of hers. She sat on atop him in her bra. *Flick.* The clasp came undone, and she slipped it off, leaving them both bare from the waist up.

Real-world, skin-to-skin rubbing was a whole lot more satisfying than the dream version. It had true texture. Scent. Taste.

He traced the line of her neck, feeling the rapid beat of her pulse. He rubbed his mouth over smooth skin to the valley between her breasts. He nuzzled her before he leaned her back, holding her that her breasts might present themselves to him, two delicious handfuls each topped with a dark berry.

His to suck. And suck he did, his mouth pulling and tugging the erect nubs while she tugged at his hair and made the most delightful fucking noises.

Her nipples weren't the only things he wanted to taste.

He flipped her and lay on the pile of leaves and discarded clothes. Downwards his mouth travelled, his fingers hooking into her pants and tugging them lower that he might kiss the flatness of her belly. He paused a moment to circle his tongue around her navel, which had her squirming and yelping his name, "Luke! That tickles."

She wiggled as he teased her one more time around the sensitive spot before moving, lowering, continuing his erotic exploration, nuzzling the soft fur covering her mound. He liked that she didn't shave. He rubbed against it, letting the smell of her surround him.

The honey scent made his mouth water and his cock swell so fucking hard. He kissed the top of her mound and whispered, "Open sesame."

She snickered, but her thighs parted for him, room enough for him to crouch between. He closed his eyes and moaned at the first lick. Actually, she moaned, too, but his was that of a man tasting the most decadent thing ever.

He lapped at her channel, his tongue parting her lips, tasting her honey. His thumb found the button of her clit and rubbed it, causing her hips to rise. Not far. He held her in his palms and continued to eat her.

To eat her until she came. His name on her lips.

"Luke. Luke." Said more deeply. "Fuck me."

Excuse me? He couldn't believe she said it. He didn't waste time. He shoved his pants down and put himself over her, taking her lips with his own, his fingers between her thighs, stroking her sex, which still rippled.

When she whimpered and cried, "More, give me more," he slammed his cock into her.

Her sex clamped down around his cock, wet and hot. The sensation exquisite.

He threw back his head and held in a howl, not wanting to scare her even as his primal side rode the surface of his skin. He fucked her harder than he planned, his body pistoning, and yet she welcomed his thrusts. Her arms wrapped around his neck, pulling him close for a kiss.

Her hips moved in time with his. Her legs wrapped around his waist. She sucked at his mouth and moaned, the vibration running through him.

"Come for me again," he encouraged with a husky murmur. "Come around my cock."

She keened, and her nails dug into his skin as she clung to him, panting and matching his rhythm. His thrusts went deeper. Harder. Faster.

Her sweet pussy tightened. Milking his dick, making each thrust so fucking tight.

"Now," she panted. "Now. Now. Now." Said on a scream as she came

And he came with her, his hot seed spilling inside her for the first time. Marking her womb. Truly making her his.

He could hold it in no longer. He howled at the pleasure of their joining. Howled and kept coming inside her, spilling all of himself in her and making her come again. Her scream was surprised and sharp.

They collapsed in a heap, sweaty bodies skin to skin. Hearts thumping fast. Best of all, she hugged him.

Brushing the hair from her temple, he kissed it softly and murmured, "Love you, Flo."

"You'd better because I'm putting all my trust in you."

And he'd make sure she wouldn't regret it.

EPILOGUE

It took them until the New Year, two months after they escaped, before they made it out of the mountains. Not that she minded. So long as she and Luke were together, they could brave anything. The man hunted a bear and made her a cloak from it— never explaining how he won with his bare hands. He always found them shelter. Crevices deep enough to build a warm fire. Shelters made of woven boughs for the times he couldn't. They even spent a glorious snowed-in week in an abandoned cabin. He kept them fed, the late fall berries sweet for picking, the birds and small game he hunted filling. Despite the harsh living conditions, she was happier than she could ever recall.

But they were always watching for hunters. Knowing what she did, she believed him when he said Chimera's people were still looking.

They'd spent some time discussing what they

should do once they exited the Rockies. She argued they should go to the media and tell his story. Show them proof and shut down Chimera and his clinic.

Luke, on the other hand, wanted to disappear. His fear was the media would ridicule them as nutjobs, but someone would listen. Someone who was part of the cover-up. He worried she would suffer an accident and he'd simply disappear.

It seemed paranoid, and yet she couldn't deny it worried her, too.

She stopped arguing the day she realized her period hadn't come since they'd fled the clinic.

That night, under stars that shone brightly, she lay on her back beside him, using his arm as a pillow. She traced the fur on his chest, noticing it was thicker than ever. Would it keep thickening?

Would he eventually become more beast than man like those creatures in the mountains?

Maybe. Luke's theory was those who escaped forgot their humanity while trying to survive. If that were the case, then it was up to her to ensure he remembered why he wanted to live.

Which was why she whispered against his skin, "I'm pregnant."

His response was a kiss and a fiercely uttered, "*They* must never know."

A month later, they were in South America, living off the grid and never going back.

Dr. Aloysius Cerberus sat across from Adrian, legs crossed, tired from a long day in the lab.

"I hear we lost another patient," Adrian noted, leaning back in his seat.

"Not yet. But if I don't halt the progression of the primacy gene, it won't be long, I'm afraid."

"There must be a way to switch it on and off."

Aloysius shrugged. "Yes, but I've yet to find it."

"We need to figure it out. The investors are asking for results." Adrian stood and paced around his desk. "Here's to hoping our other project pans out."

"Where are Luke and the nurse now?"

"South America." Adrian held up his phone and tapped the screen a few times. The monitor on the wall lit up, a large map of the world filling it. On it, blinking dots. Some clustered in Canada, the Rockies to be specific, which was their clinic. More in Europe and Mexico. Plus a few strays. The screen zoomed into a spot in South America where two dots pulsed.

"Is that them?"

"Yes. Their chips are transmitting their vitals twice a day when our satellites go past. They'll have to be closely monitored."

"Because?"

"She's pregnant."

Aloysius clapped his hands. "That's wonderful news. When are you planning to bring them back in?"

"Not yet. I don't want to make the same mistake we made with Samuel and Delilah." That ended in a tragedy that saw them lose not only two viable subjects but the child, too.

"What about monitoring the pregnancy?"

Adrian tucked his hands behind his back. "We're going to let nature do its thing and watch from afar. I didn't put them through that charade to bring them back too soon."

Because all along Adrian had planned for Luke to bond with the nurse. All of it, from their shared dreams, to their bond—which was chemically induced —to their escape, all orchestrated with one goal in mind.

Breeding.

Because much like zoo animals, the patients didn't procreate well or successfully when kept in close quarters.

"What if the child proves dangerous in the womb?"

Adrian's smile was tight and cold. "Then I guess we'll collect our wolfman and try again.

IT HAD BEEN A WEEK SINCE BECKY HAD SEEN Margaret. The woman had upped and disappeared overnight, as had her patient Luke. The rumor going around said they ran off. Management claimed she was let go for misconduct.

Whatever the reason, Becky missed her. Wished she'd been nicer those last few times because she could have used a friend. Especially now.

Becky stood on the shore of the lake, shivering despite the sun. For the past few days she'd been running a fever. A cold one, which made no sense. Her core temperature kept dropping, and her skin itched. Itched something fierce. And she craved water. Not to drink.

Nope. She wanted to soak in it. Took crazy long showers and still wasn't satisfied.

Which was how she found herself on the shore.

The lake had always intimidated her. Yet it kept calling. Standing on the shore, on the only tiny section of shallow beach, she kicked off her shoes and dipped her toes into the water. The cold barely registered. So she waded deeper and deeper until the bottom dropped away. She went under, body, face. She sank, eyes wide as she suddenly realized her peril.

Panic clawed at her as her lungs tightened. And when she could handle it no more, she opened her mouth and let it in.

FIND OUT WHAT HAPPENS NEXT IN GUARDING THE MERMAID

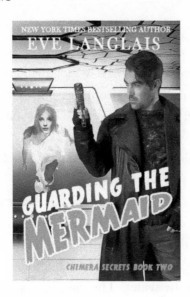

For more books by Eve Langlais or to receive her newsletter, please visit

EveLanglais.com